11/14

W9-AUI-994

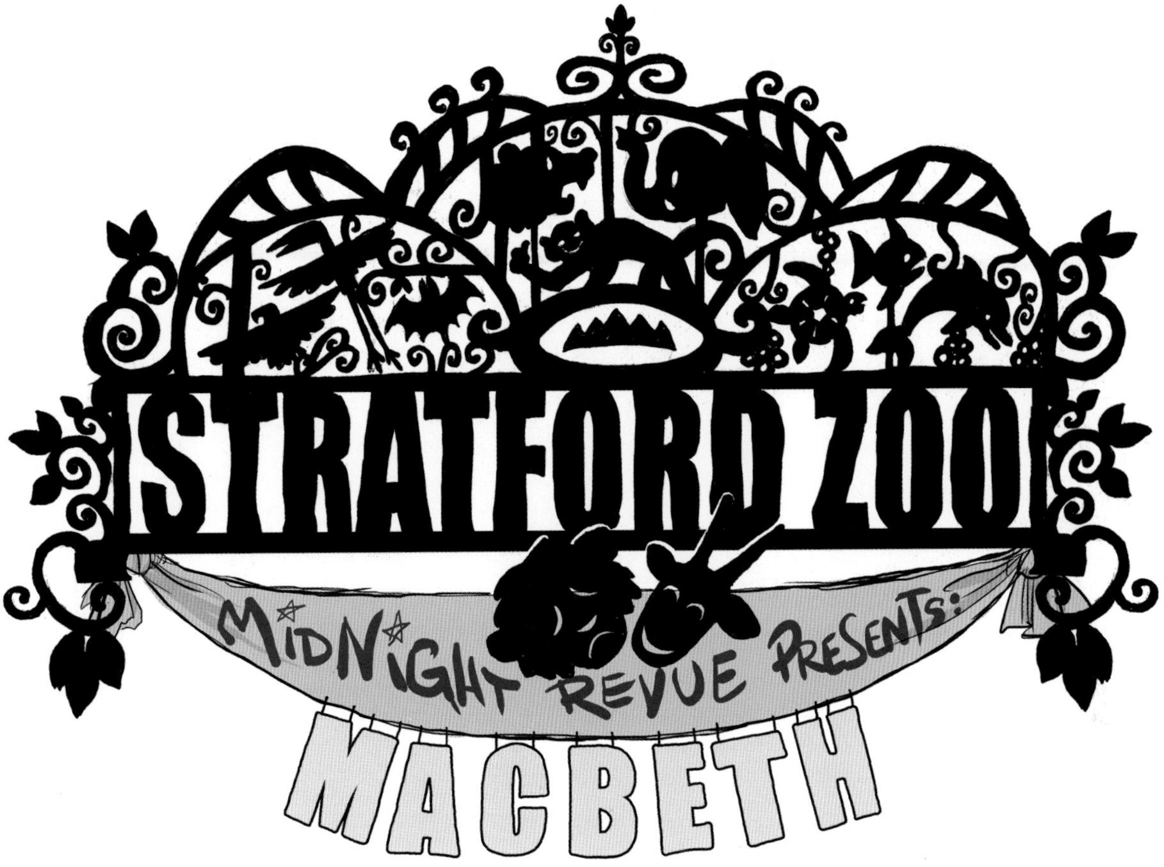
STRATFORD ZOO
MIDNIGHT REVUE PRESENTS:
MACBETH

STRATFORD ZOO

MIDNIGHT REVUE PRESENTS:

MACBETH

Written by Ian Lendler
Art by Zack Giallongo
Colors by Alisa Harris

First Second
New York

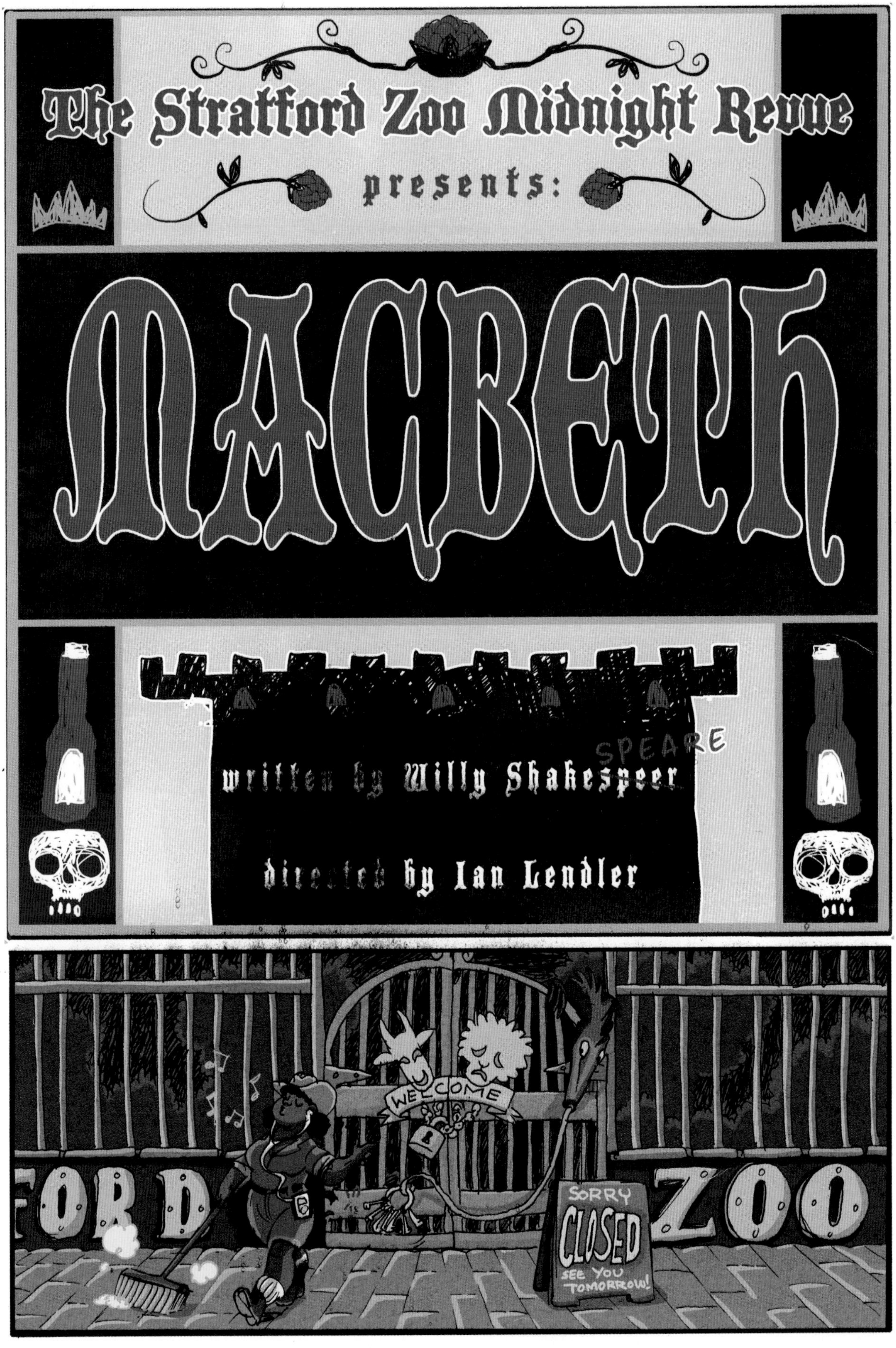
The Stratford Zoo Midnight Revue
presents:
MACBETH
written by Willy Shakespeer
SPEARE
directed by Ian Lendler
WELCOME
FORD
ZOO
SORRY
CLOSED
SEE YOU TOMORROW!

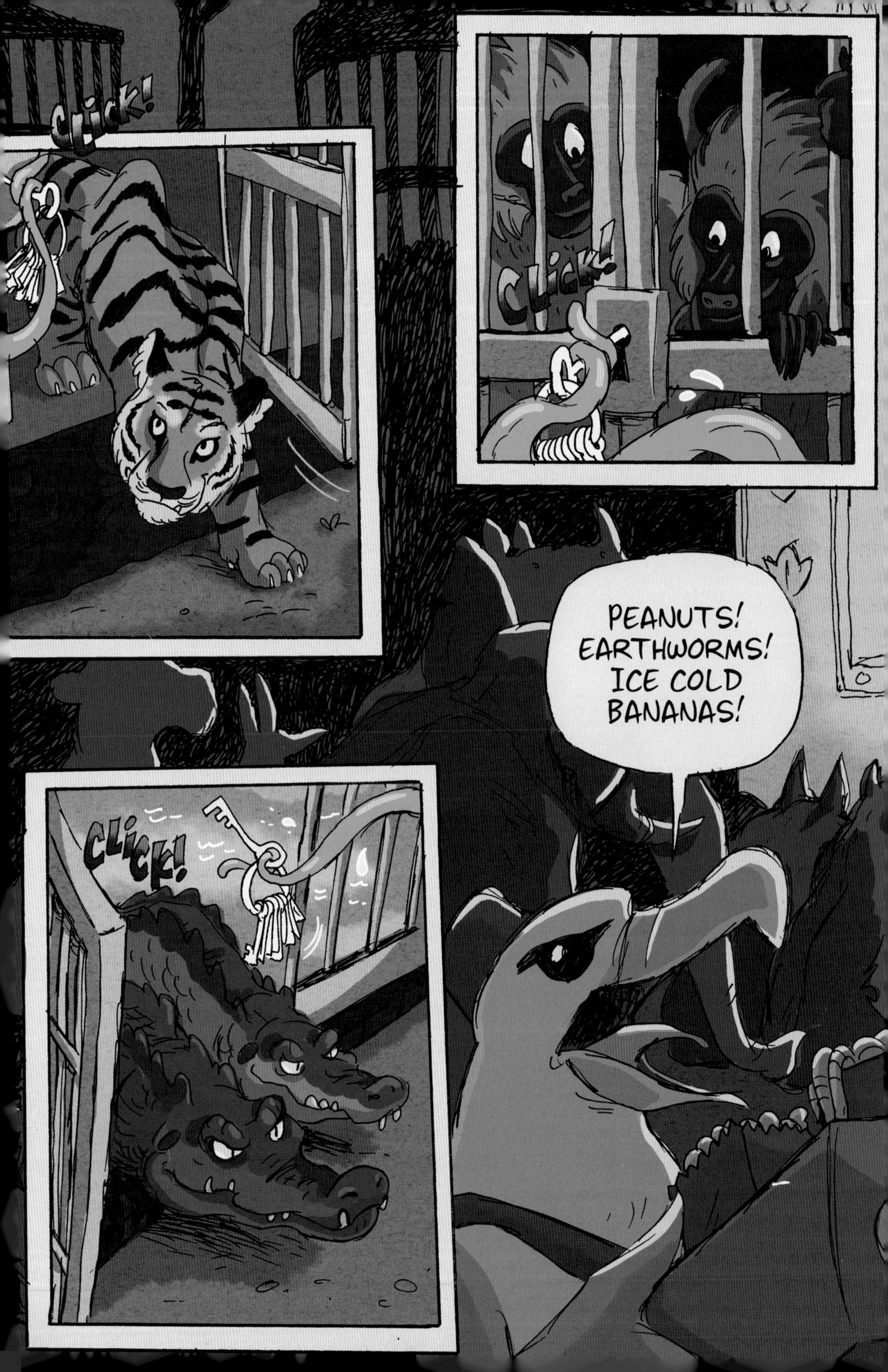
CLICK!
CLICK!
PEANUTS! EARTHWORMS! ICE COLD BANANAS!
CLICK!

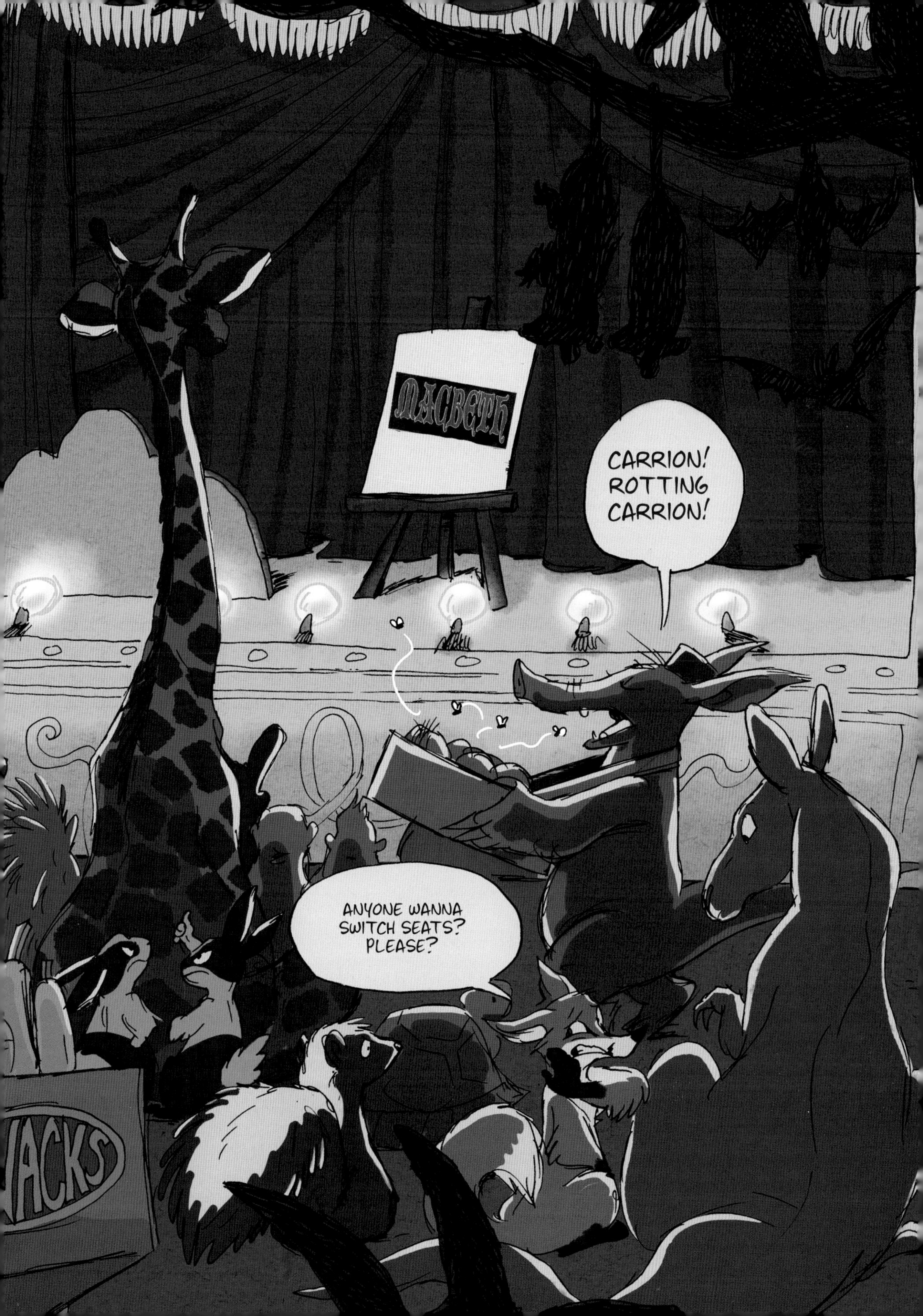
MACBETH
CARRION! ROTTING CARRION!
ANYONE WANNA SWITCH SEATS? PLEASE?

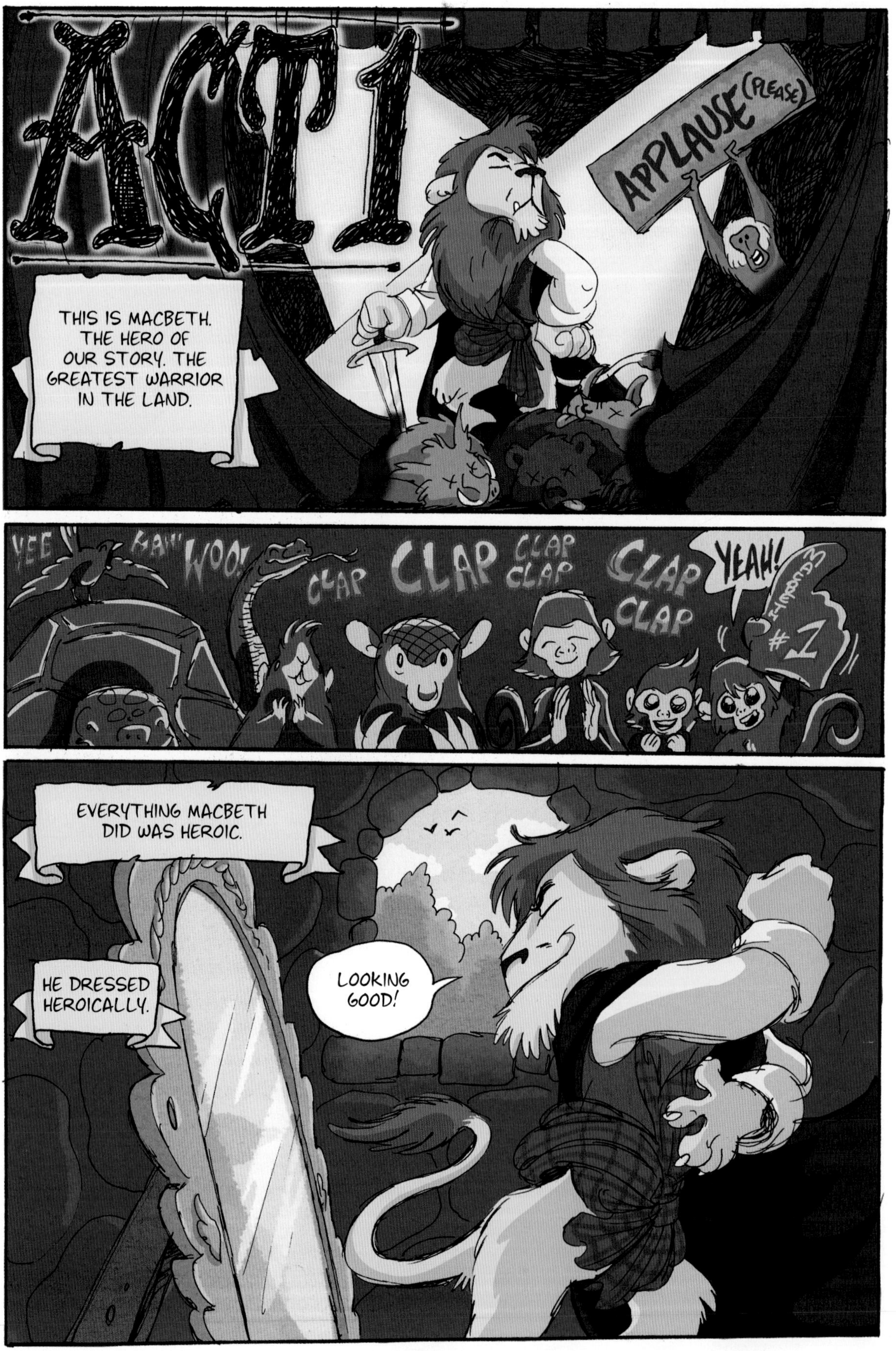
ACT 1
APPLAUSE (PLEASE)
THIS IS MACBETH. THE HERO OF OUR STORY. THE GREATEST WARRIOR IN THE LAND.
YEE HAW WOO!
CLAP CLAP CLAP CLAP CLAP CLAP
YEAH!
#1
EVERYTHING MACBETH DID WAS HEROIC.
HE DRESSED HEROICALLY.
LOOKING GOOD!

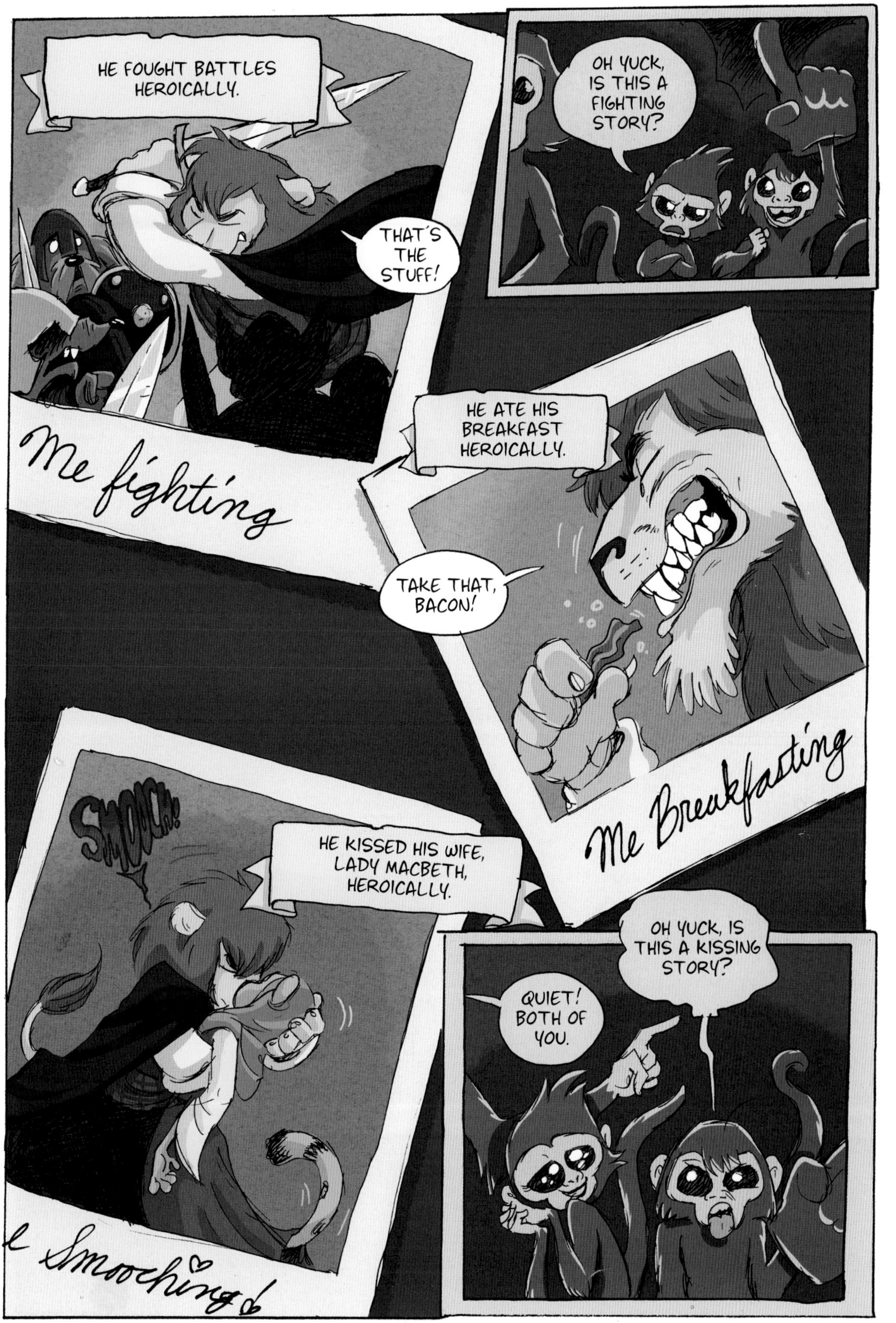
HE FOUGHT BATTLES HEROICALLY.
THAT'S THE STUFF!
Me fighting
OH YUCK, IS THIS A FIGHTING STORY?
HE ATE HIS BREAKFAST HEROICALLY.
TAKE THAT, BACON!
Me Breakfasting
HE KISSED HIS WIFE, LADY MACBETH, HEROICALLY.
SMOOCH!
& Smooching!
OH YUCK, IS THIS A KISSING STORY?
QUIET! BOTH OF YOU.

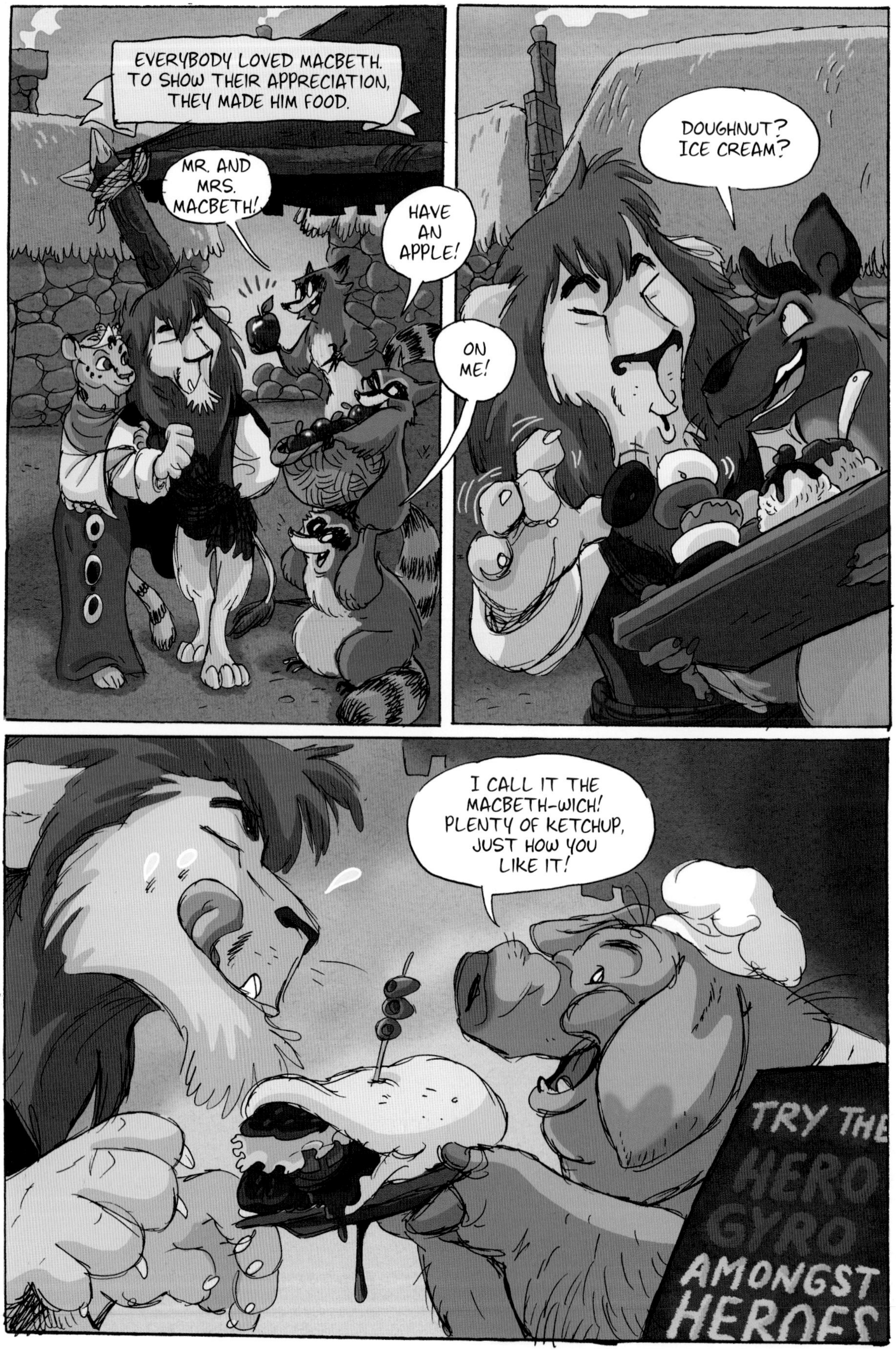
EVERYBODY LOVED MACBETH. TO SHOW THEIR APPRECIATION, THEY MADE HIM FOOD.
MR. AND MRS. MACBETH!
HAVE AN APPLE!
ON ME!
DOUGHNUT? ICE CREAM?
I CALL IT THE MACBETH-WICH! PLENTY OF KETCHUP, JUST HOW YOU LIKE IT!
TRY THE
HERO
GYRO
AMONGST

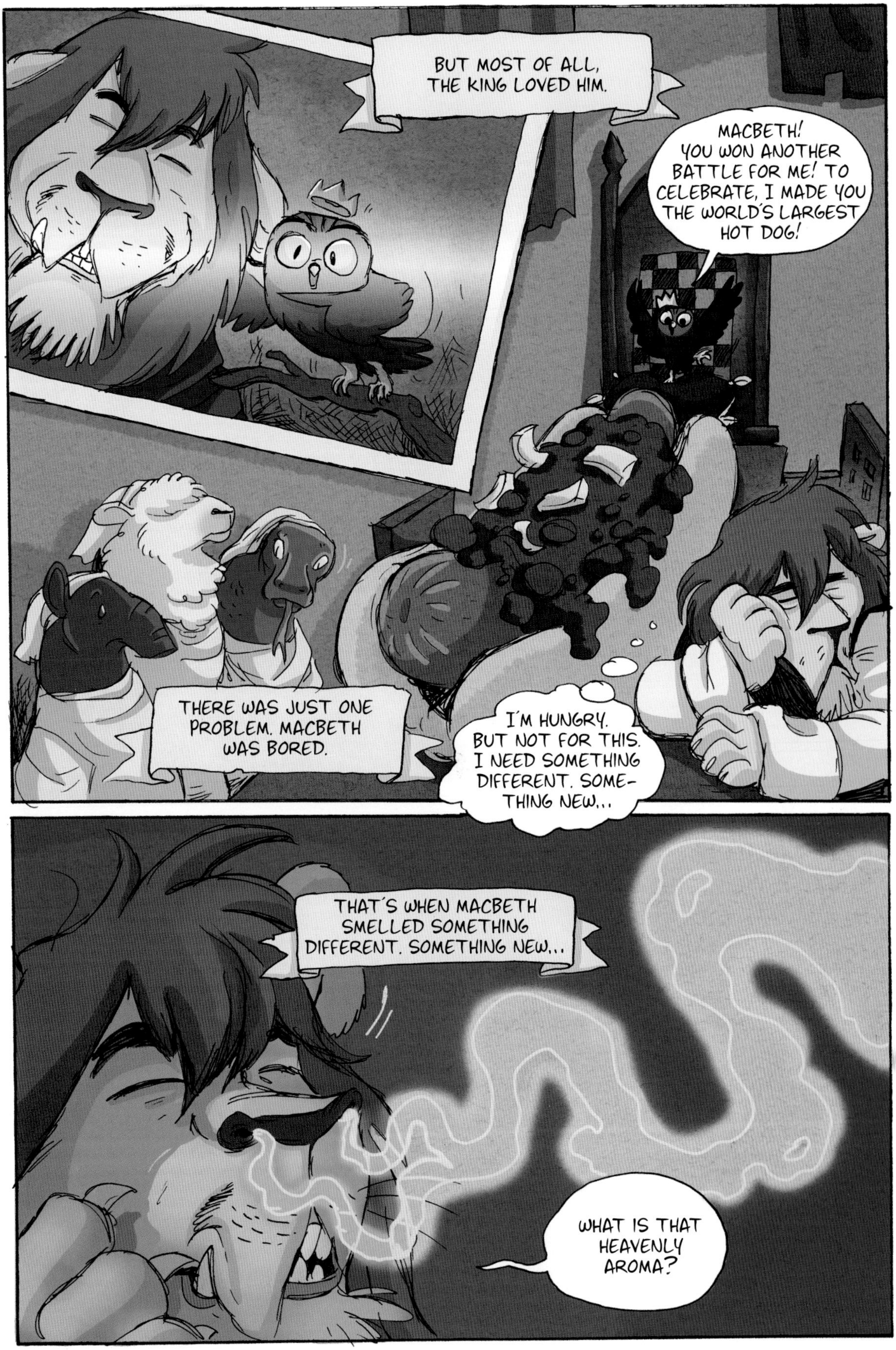
BUT MOST OF ALL, THE KING LOVED HIM.
MACBETH! YOU WON ANOTHER BATTLE FOR ME! TO CELEBRATE, I MADE YOU THE WORLD'S LARGEST HOT DOG!
THERE WAS JUST ONE PROBLEM. MACBETH WAS BORED.
I'M HUNGRY. BUT NOT FOR THIS. I NEED SOMETHING DIFFERENT. SOME-THING NEW...
THAT'S WHEN MACBETH SMELLED SOMETHING DIFFERENT. SOMETHING NEW...
WHAT IS THAT HEAVENLY AROMA?

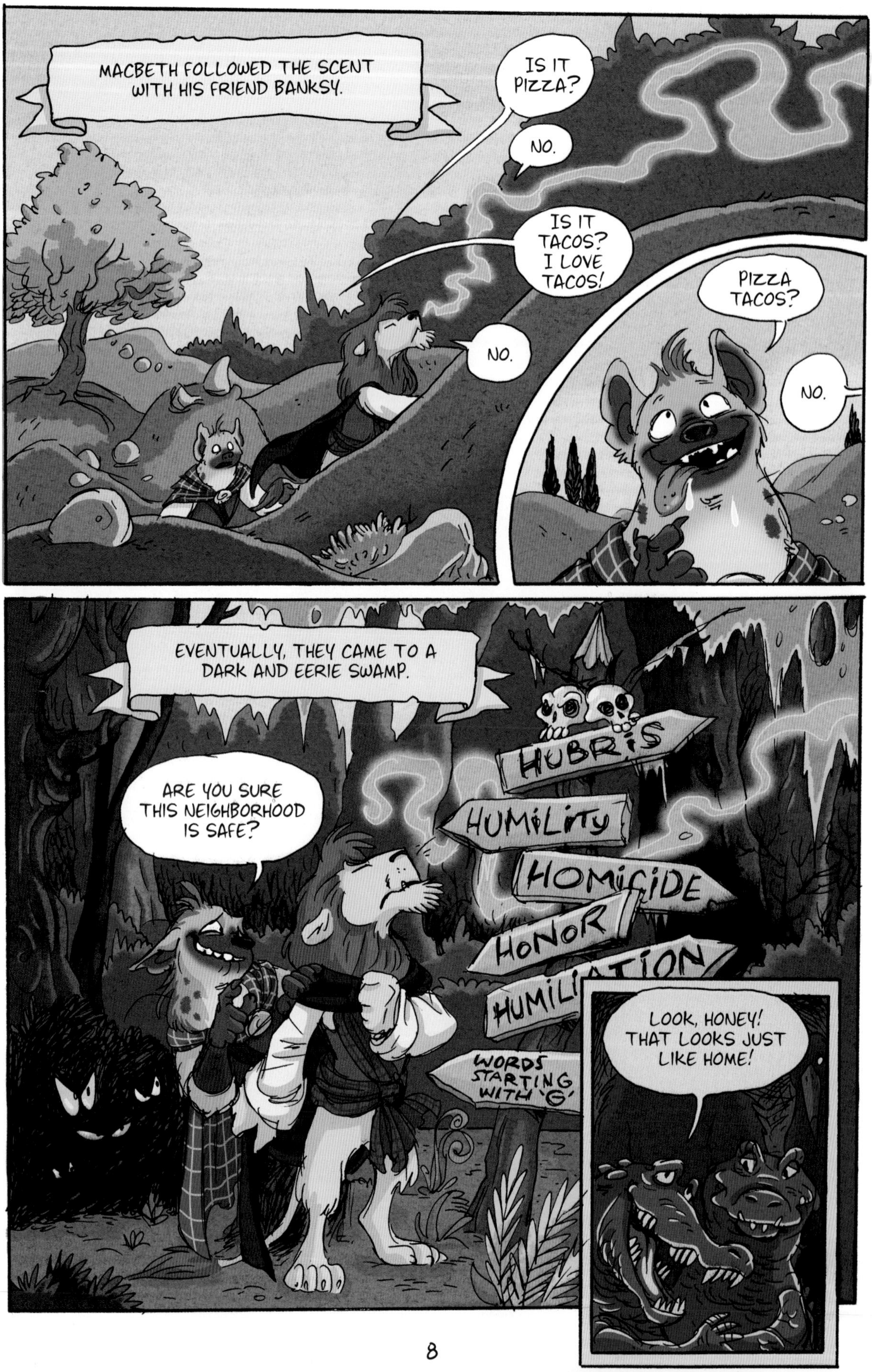
MACBETH FOLLOWED THE SCENT WITH HIS FRIEND BANKSY.
IS IT PIZZA?
NO.
IS IT TACOS? I LOVE TACOS!
NO.
PIZZA TACOS?
NO.
EVENTUALLY, THEY CAME TO A DARK AND EERIE SWAMP.
HUBRIS
HUMILITY
HOMICIDE
HONOR
HUMILIATION
WORDS STARTING WITH 'G'
ARE YOU SURE THIS NEIGHBORHOOD IS SAFE?
LOOK, HONEY! THAT LOOKS JUST LIKE HOME!

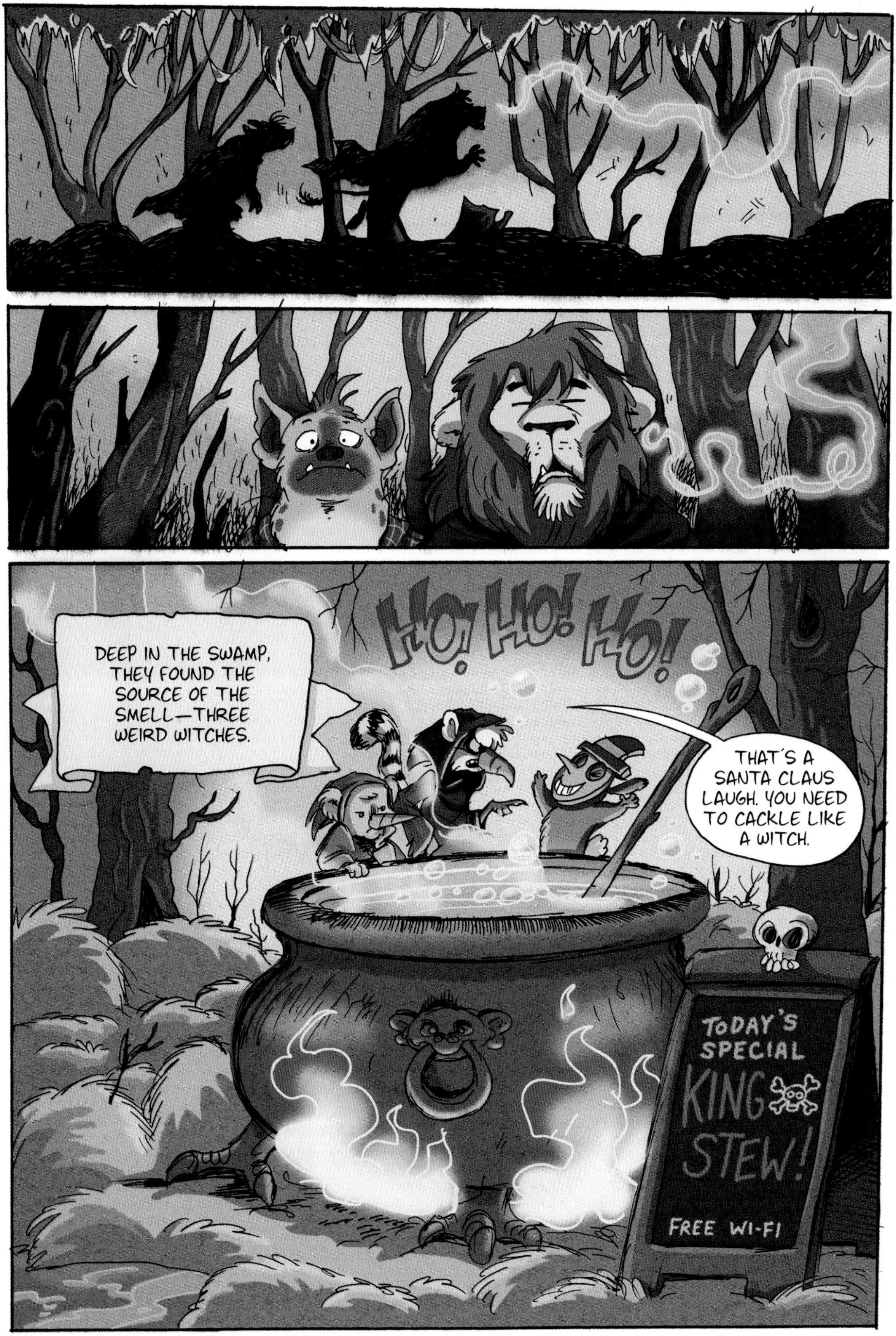
DEEP IN THE SWAMP, THEY FOUND THE SOURCE OF THE SMELL—THREE WEIRD WITCHES.
HO! HO! HO!
THAT'S A SANTA CLAUS LAUGH. YOU NEED TO CACKLE LIKE A WITCH.
TODAY'S SPECIAL
KING STEW!
FREE WI-FI

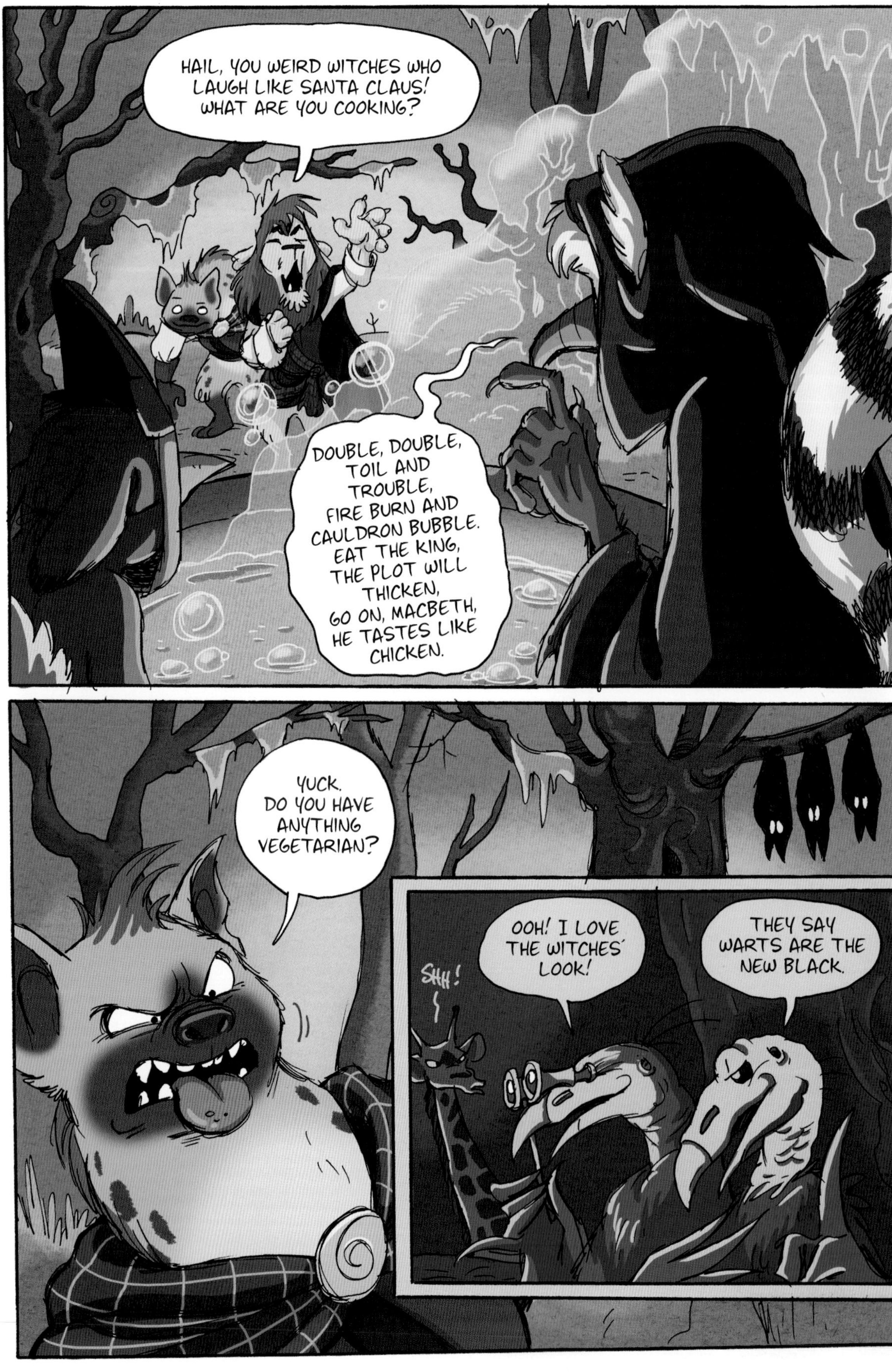
HAIL, YOU WEIRD WITCHES WHO LAUGH LIKE SANTA CLAUS! WHAT ARE YOU COOKING?
DOUBLE, DOUBLE, TOIL AND TROUBLE, FIRE BURN AND CAULDRON BUBBLE. EAT THE KING, THE PLOT WILL THICKEN, GO ON, MACBETH, HE TASTES LIKE CHICKEN.
YUCK. DO YOU HAVE ANYTHING VEGETARIAN?
SHH!
OOH! I LOVE THE WITCHES' LOOK!
THEY SAY WARTS ARE THE NEW BLACK.

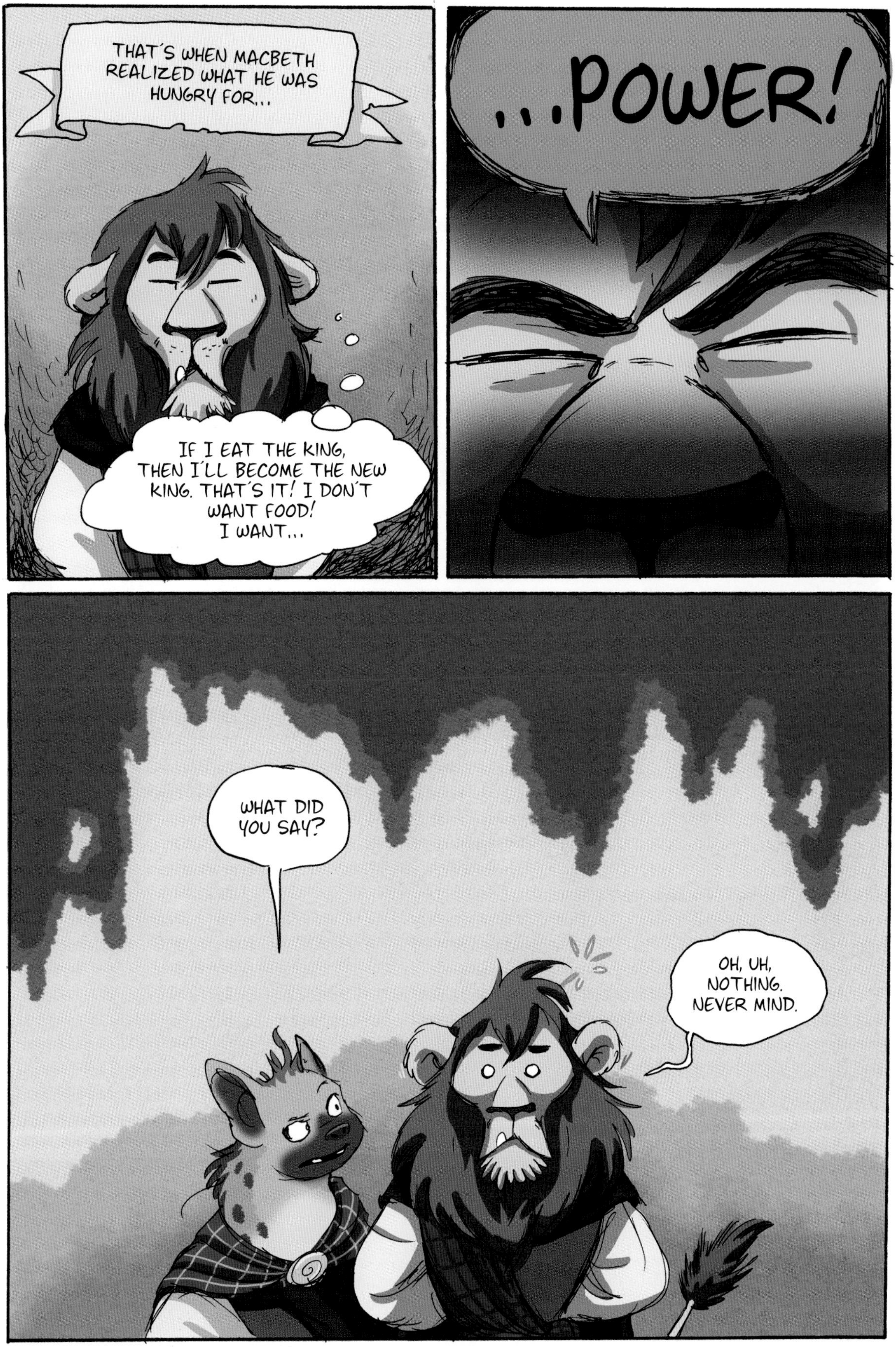
THAT'S WHEN MACBETH REALIZED WHAT HE WAS HUNGRY FOR...
IF I EAT THE KING, THEN I'LL BECOME THE NEW KING. THAT'S IT! I DON'T WANT FOOD! I WANT...
...POWER!
WHAT DID YOU SAY?
OH, UH, NOTHING. NEVER MIND.

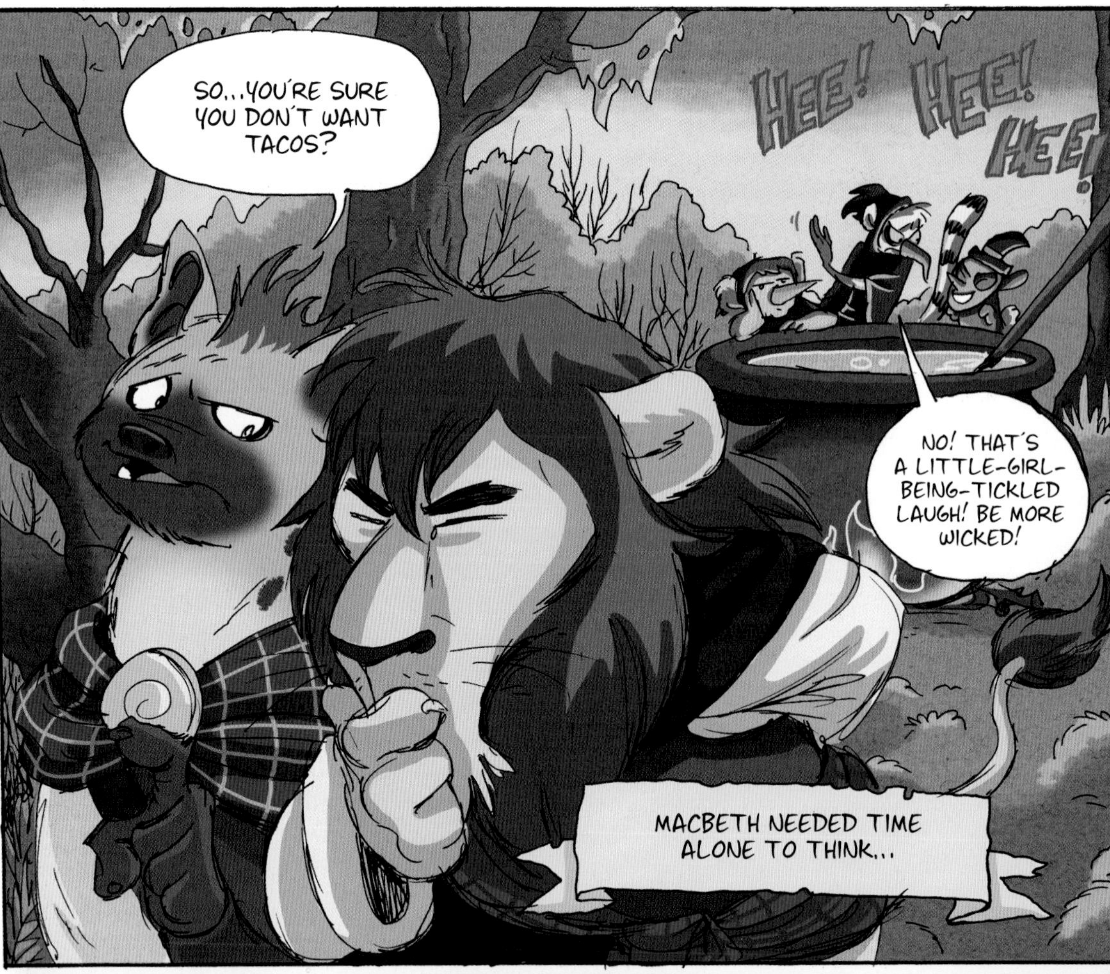
SO... YOU'RE SURE YOU DON'T WANT TACOS?
HEE! HEE! HEE!
NO! THAT'S A LITTLE-GIRL-BEING-TICKLED LAUGH! BE MORE WICKED!
MACBETH NEEDED TIME ALONE TO THINK...

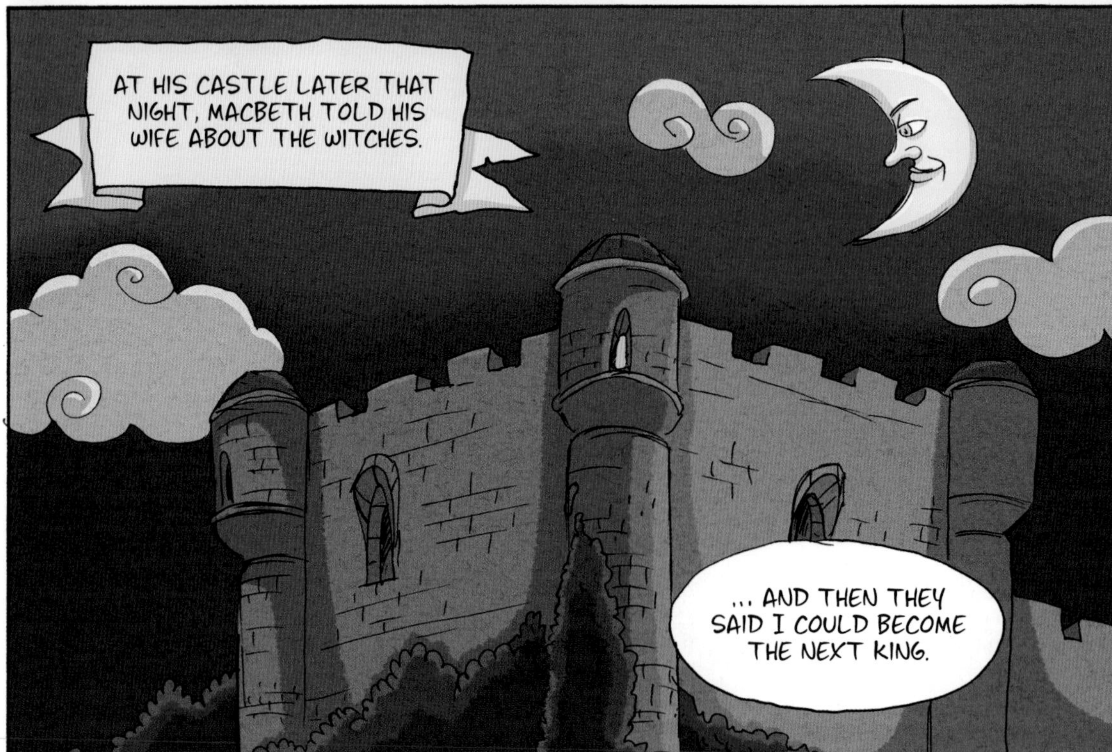
AT HIS CASTLE LATER THAT NIGHT, MACBETH TOLD HIS WIFE ABOUT THE WITCHES.
... AND THEN THEY SAID I COULD BECOME THE NEXT KING.

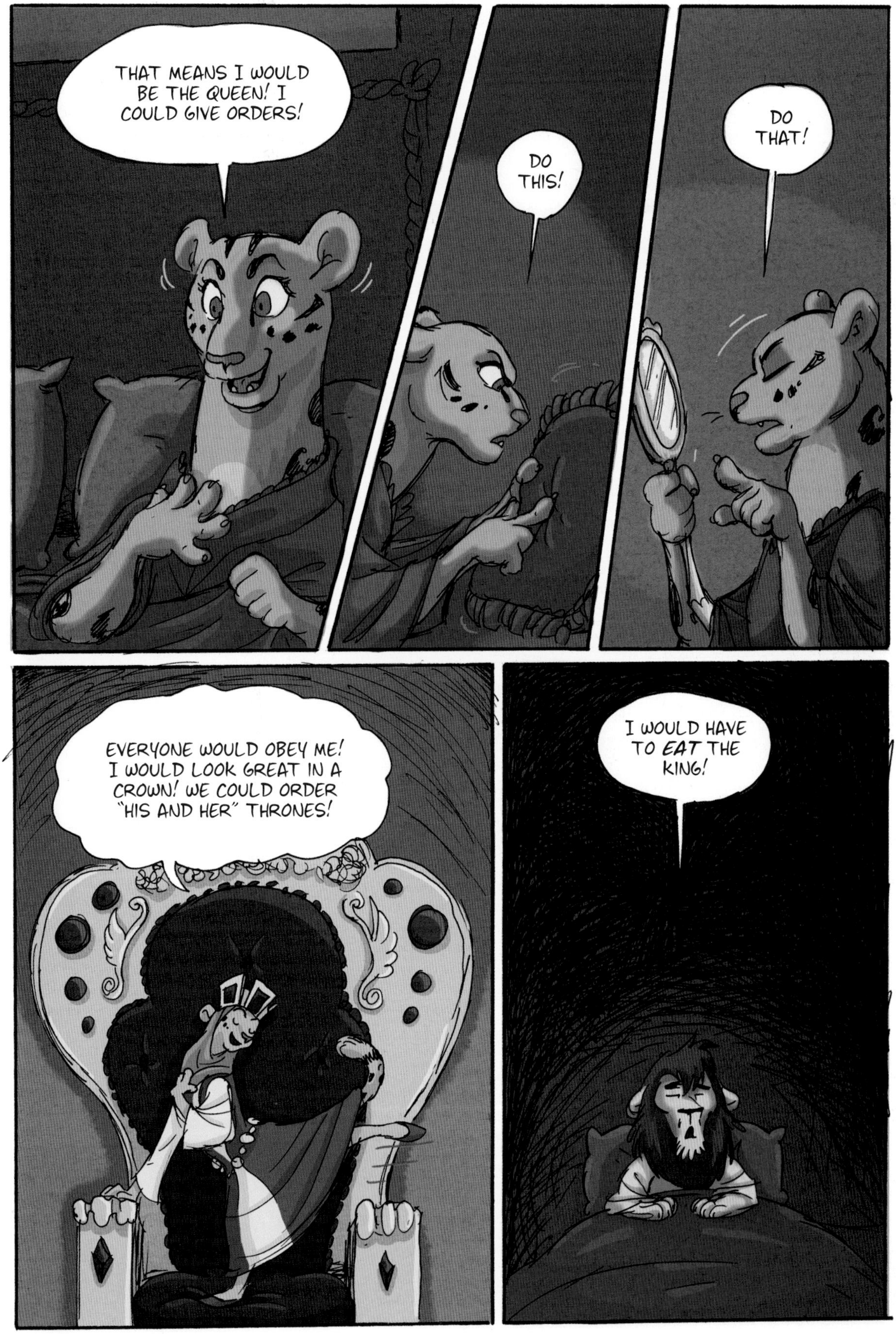
THAT MEANS I WOULD BE THE QUEEN! I COULD GIVE ORDERS!
DO THIS!
DO THAT!
EVERYONE WOULD OBEY ME! I WOULD LOOK GREAT IN A CROWN! WE COULD ORDER "HIS AND HER" THRONES!
I WOULD HAVE TO *EAT* THE KING!

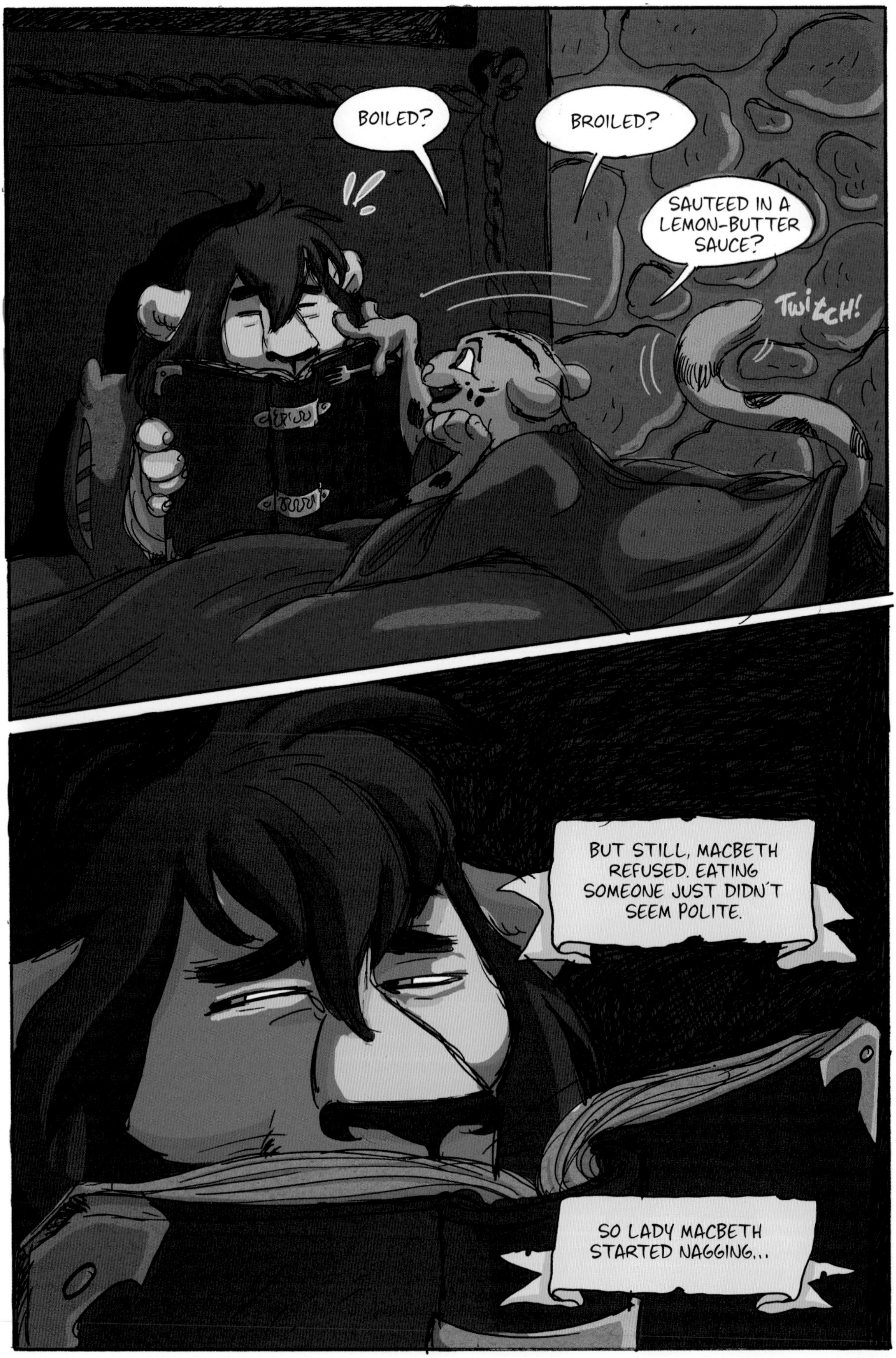
BOILED?
BROILED?
SAUTEED IN A LEMON-BUTTER SAUCE?
TWITCH!
BUT STILL, MACBETH REFUSED. EATING SOMEONE JUST DIDN'T SEEM POLITE.
SO LADY MACBETH STARTED NAGGING...

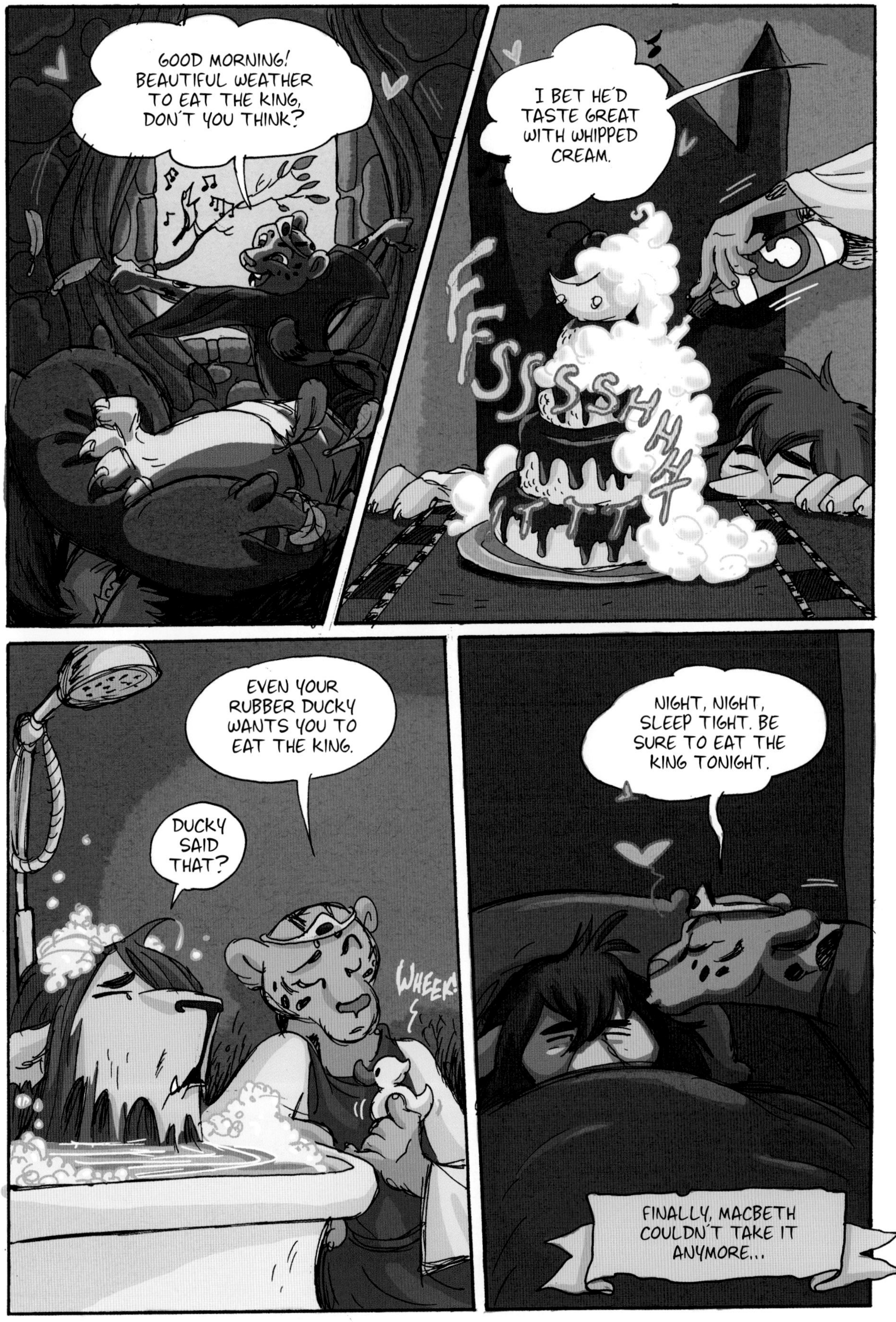
GOOD MORNING! BEAUTIFUL WEATHER TO EAT THE KING, DON´T YOU THINK?
I BET HE´D TASTE GREAT WITH WHIPPED CREAM.
FFSSSSHHHT
EVEN YOUR RUBBER DUCKY WANTS YOU TO EAT THE KING.
DUCKY SAID THAT?
WHEEK!
NIGHT, NIGHT, SLEEP TIGHT. BE SURE TO EAT THE KING TONIGHT.
FINALLY, MACBETH COULDN´T TAKE IT ANYMORE...

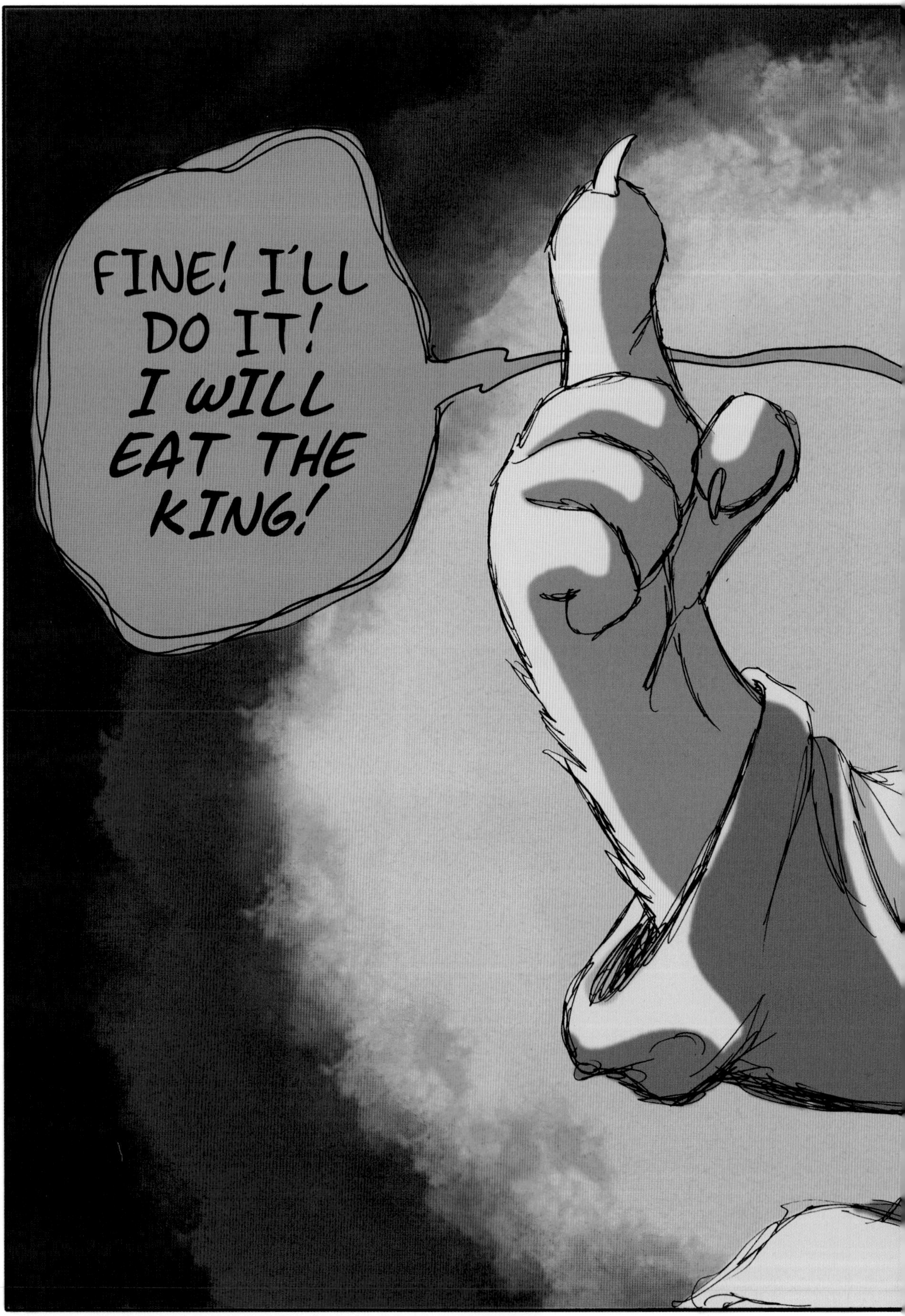
FINE! I'LL DO IT! I WILL EAT THE KING!

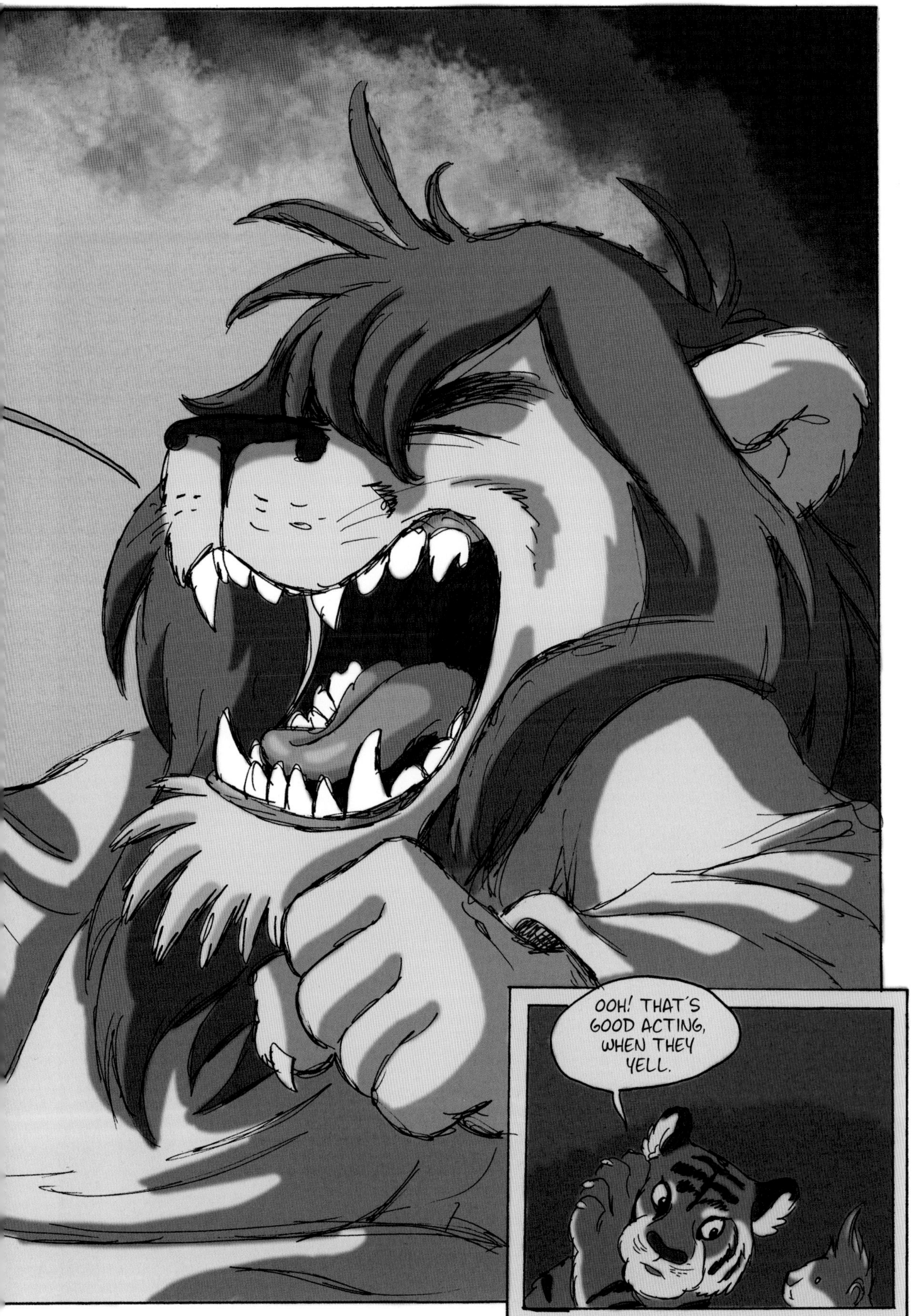
OOH! THAT'S GOOD ACTING, WHEN THEY YELL.

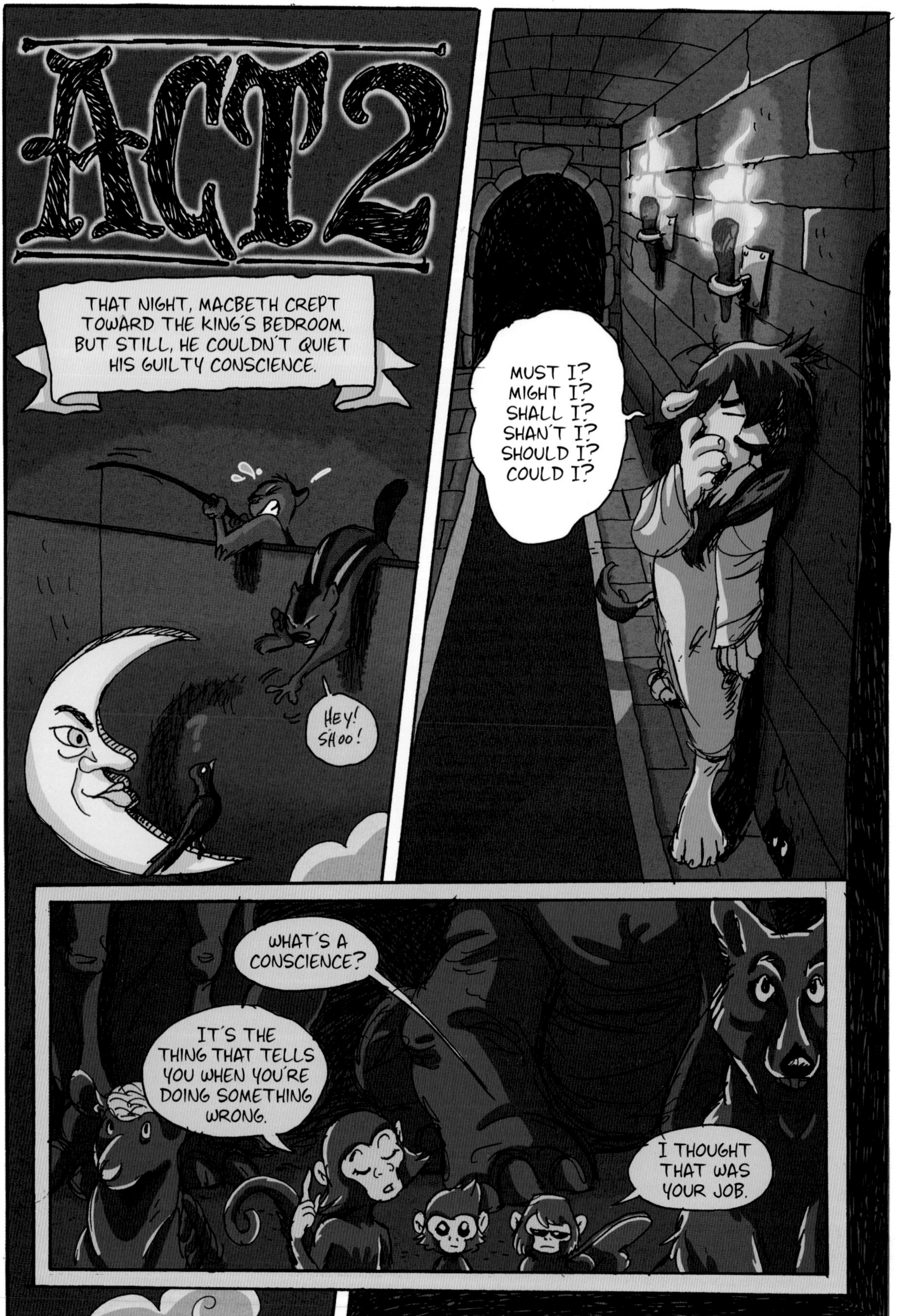

ACT 2
THAT NIGHT, MACBETH CREPT TOWARD THE KING'S BEDROOM. BUT STILL, HE COULDN'T QUIET HIS GUILTY CONSCIENCE.
HEY! SHOO!
MUST I? MIGHT I? SHALL I? SHAN'T I? SHOULD I? COULD I?
WHAT'S A CONSCIENCE?
IT'S THE THING THAT TELLS YOU WHEN YOU'RE DOING SOMETHING WRONG.
I THOUGHT THAT WAS YOUR JOB.

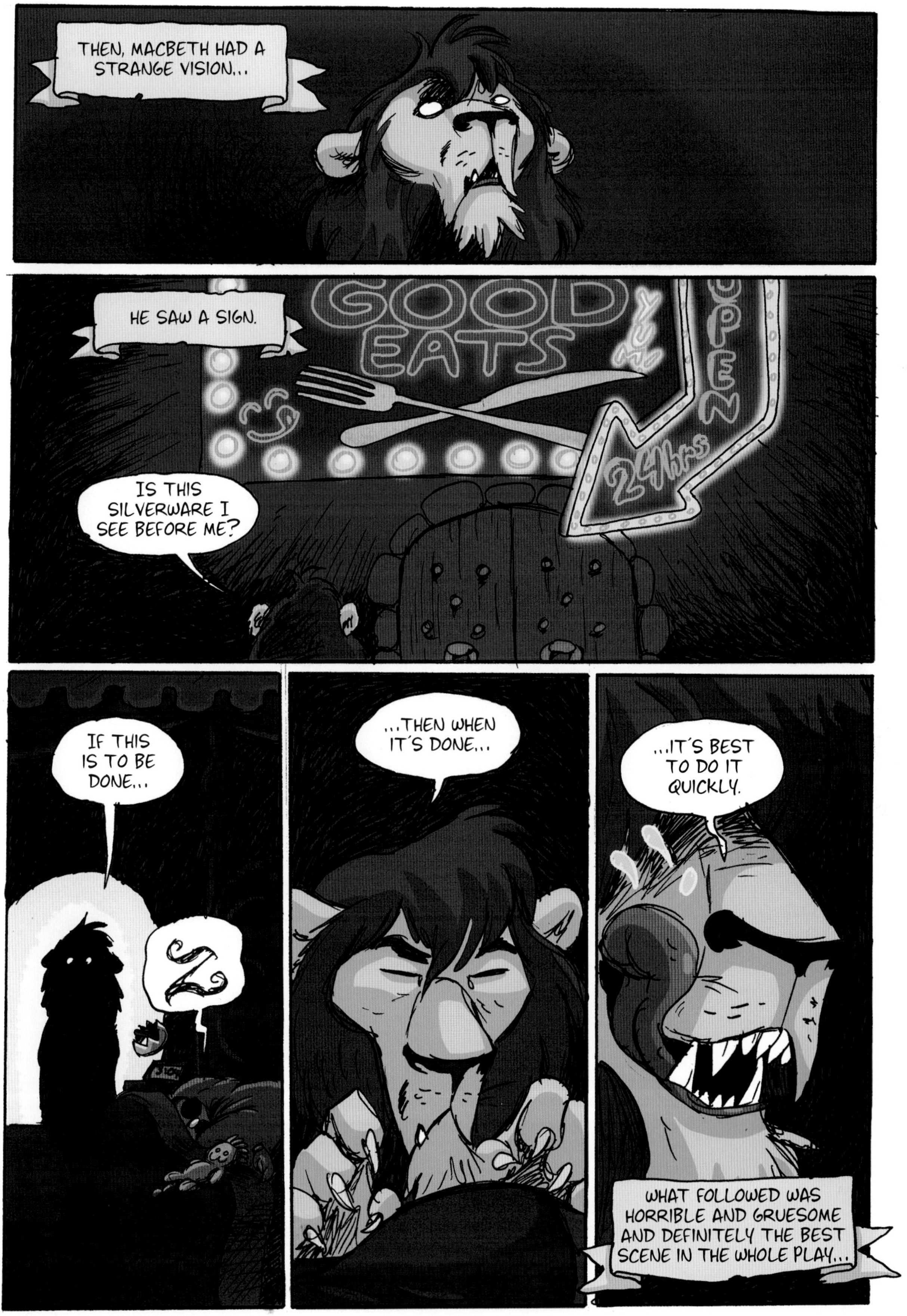

THEN, MACBETH HAD A STRANGE VISION...
HE SAW A SIGN.
GOOD EATS
OPEN
24hrs
IS THIS SILVERWARE I SEE BEFORE ME?
IF THIS IS TO BE DONE...
Z
...THEN WHEN IT'S DONE...
...IT'S BEST TO DO IT QUICKLY.
WHAT FOLLOWED WAS HORRIBLE AND GRUESOME AND DEFINITELY THE BEST SCENE IN THE WHOLE PLAY...

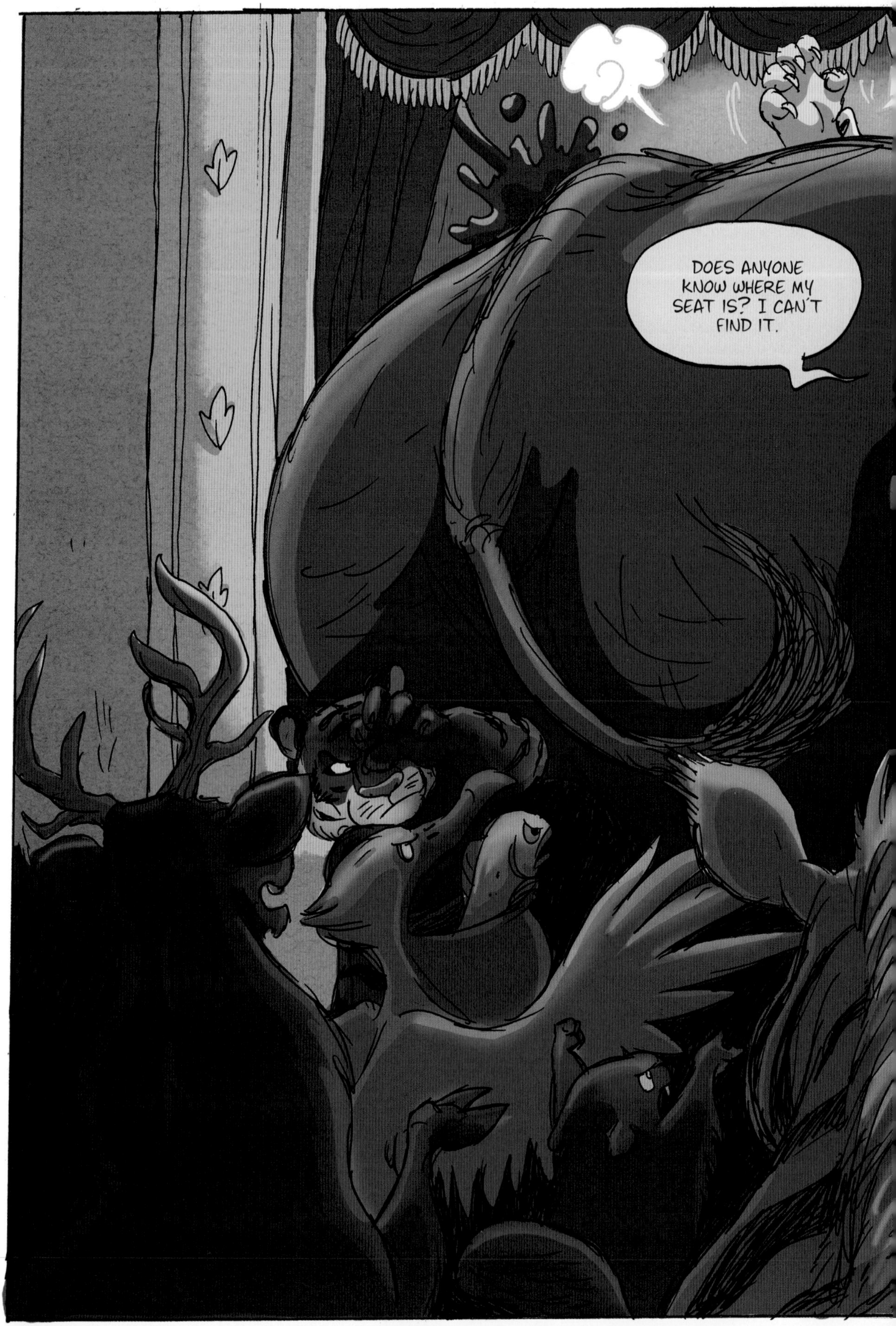
DOES ANYONE KNOW WHERE MY SEAT IS? I CAN'T FIND IT.

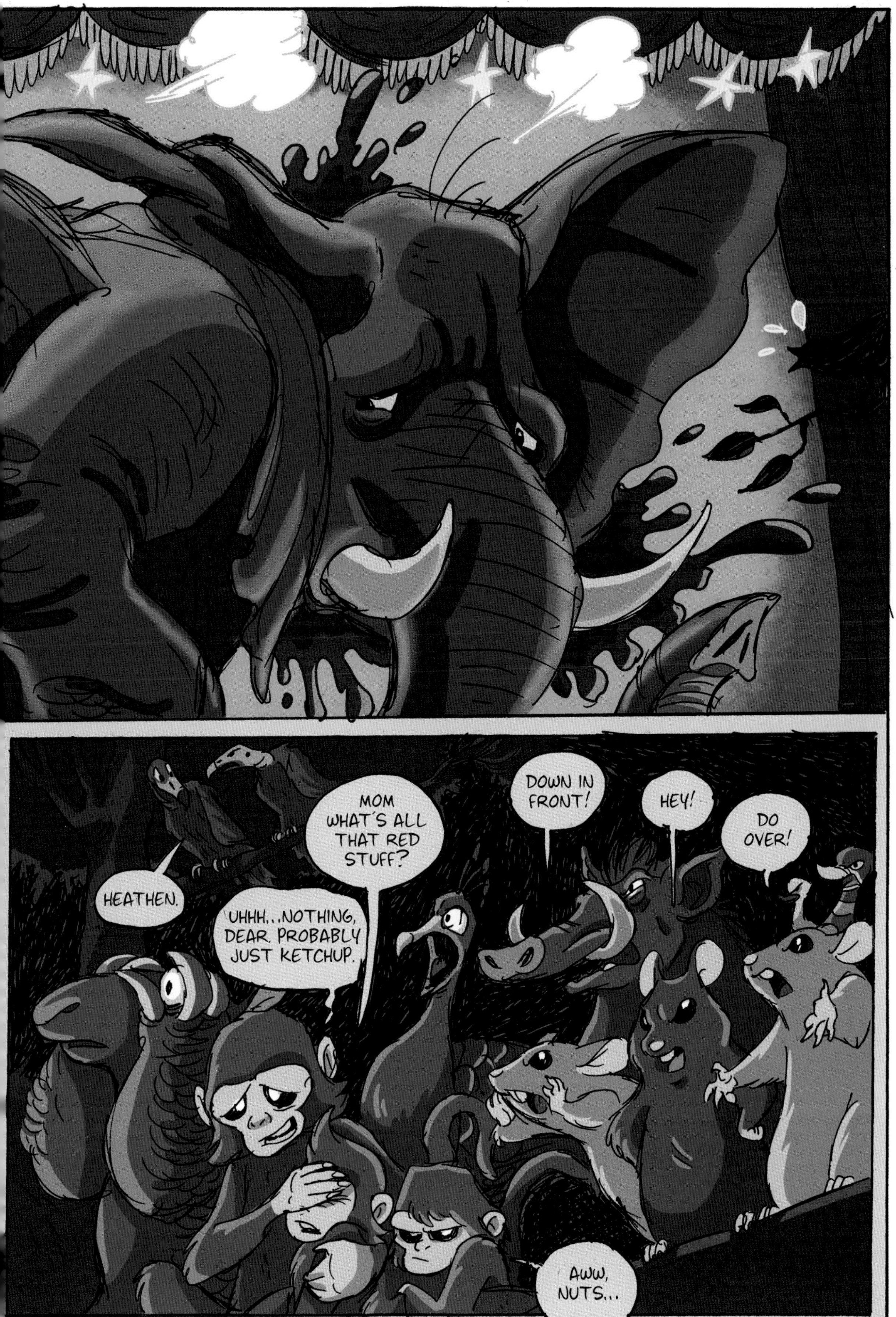
HEATHEN.
MOM WHAT'S ALL THAT RED STUFF?
UHHH...NOTHING, DEAR. PROBABLY JUST KETCHUP.
DOWN IN FRONT!
HEY!
DO OVER!
AWW, NUTS...

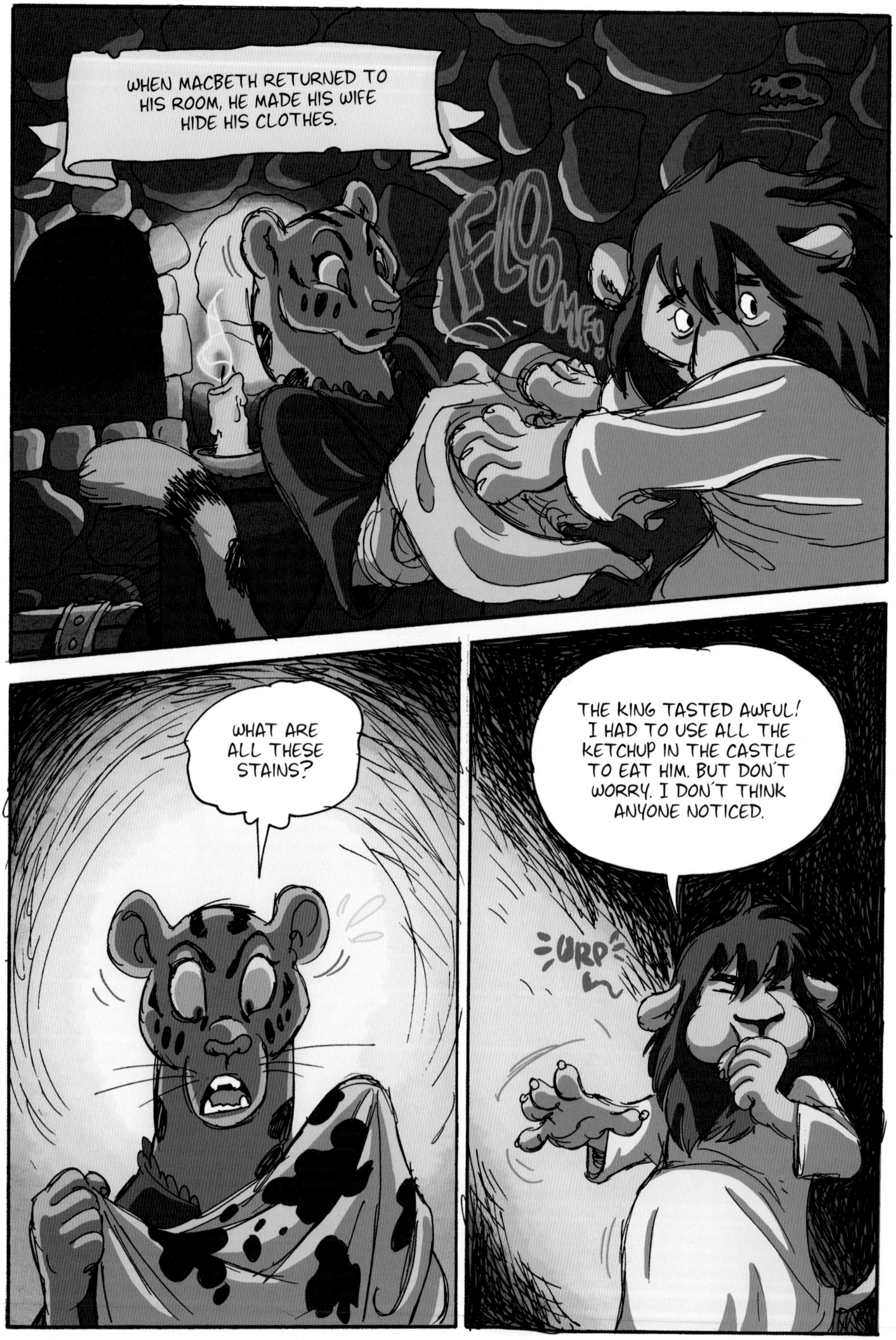
WHEN MACBETH RETURNED TO HIS ROOM, HE MADE HIS WIFE HIDE HIS CLOTHES.
FLOOMF!
WHAT ARE ALL THESE STAINS?
THE KING TASTED AWFUL! I HAD TO USE ALL THE KETCHUP IN THE CASTLE TO EAT HIM. BUT DON'T WORRY. I DON'T THINK ANYONE NOTICED.
URP

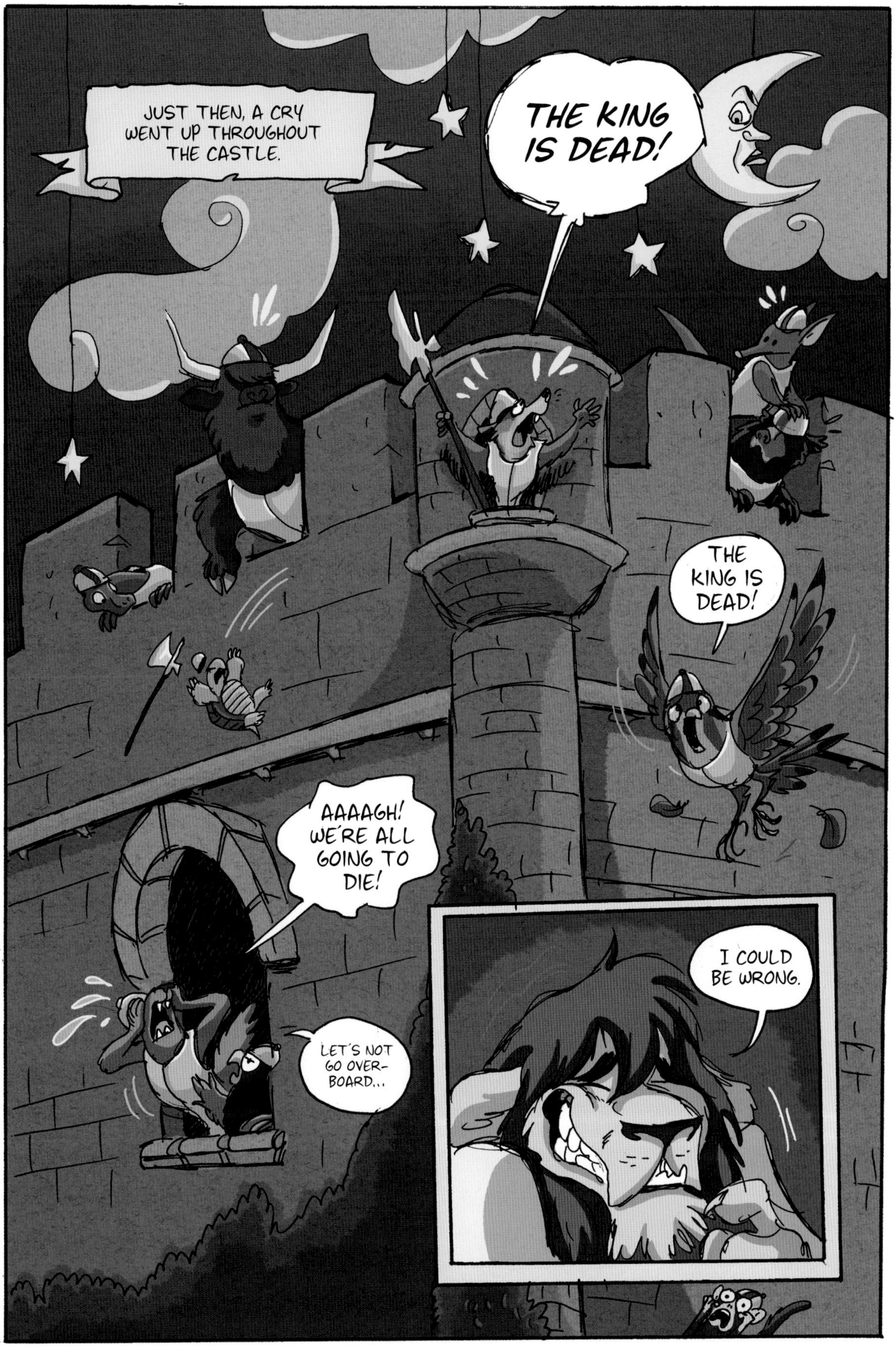
JUST THEN, A CRY WENT UP THROUGHOUT THE CASTLE.
THE KING IS DEAD!
THE KING IS DEAD!
AAAAGH! WE'RE ALL GOING TO DIE!
LET'S NOT GO OVER-BOARD...
I COULD BE WRONG.

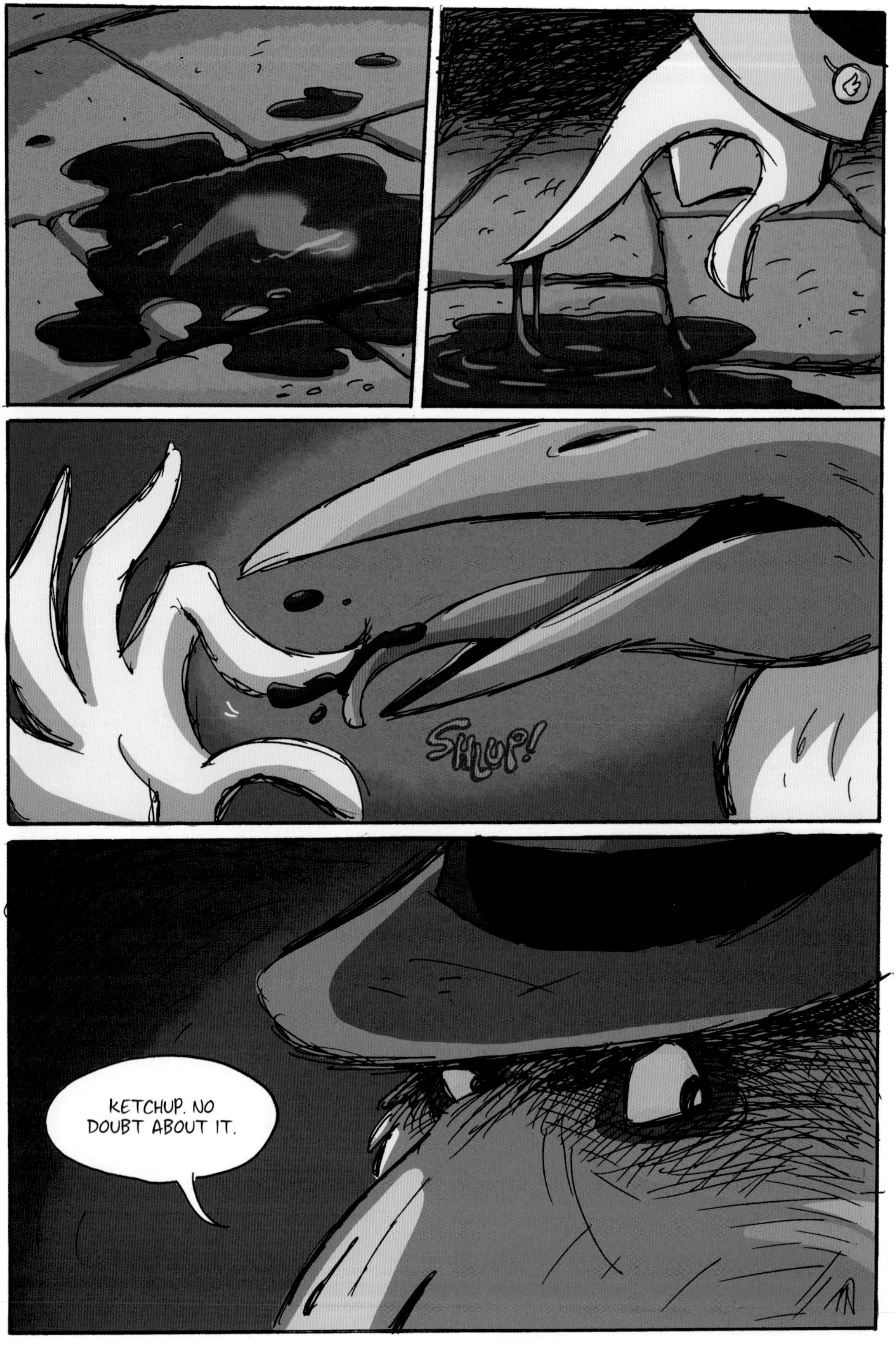
SHLUP!
KETCHUP. NO DOUBT ABOUT IT.

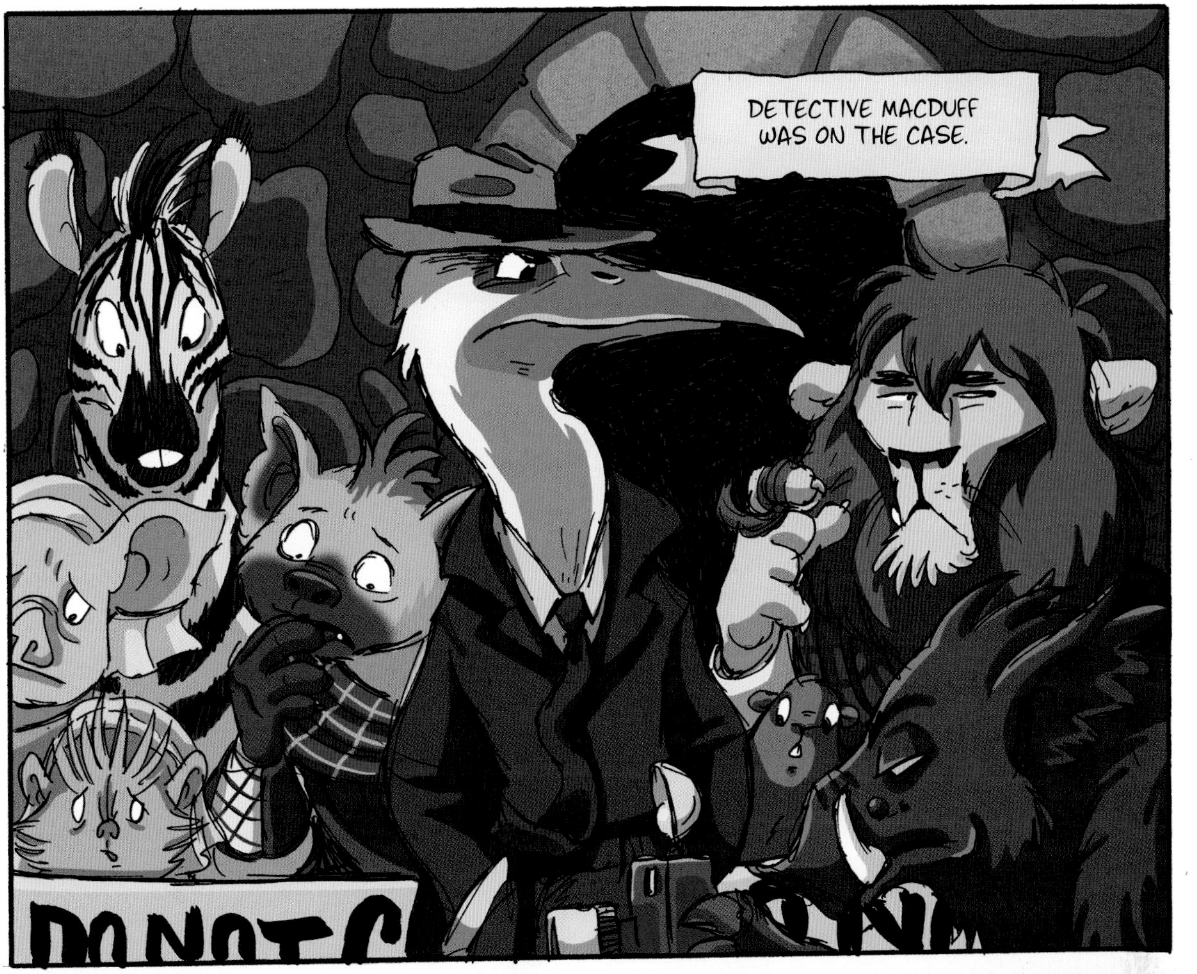
DETECTIVE MACDUFF WAS ON THE CASE.

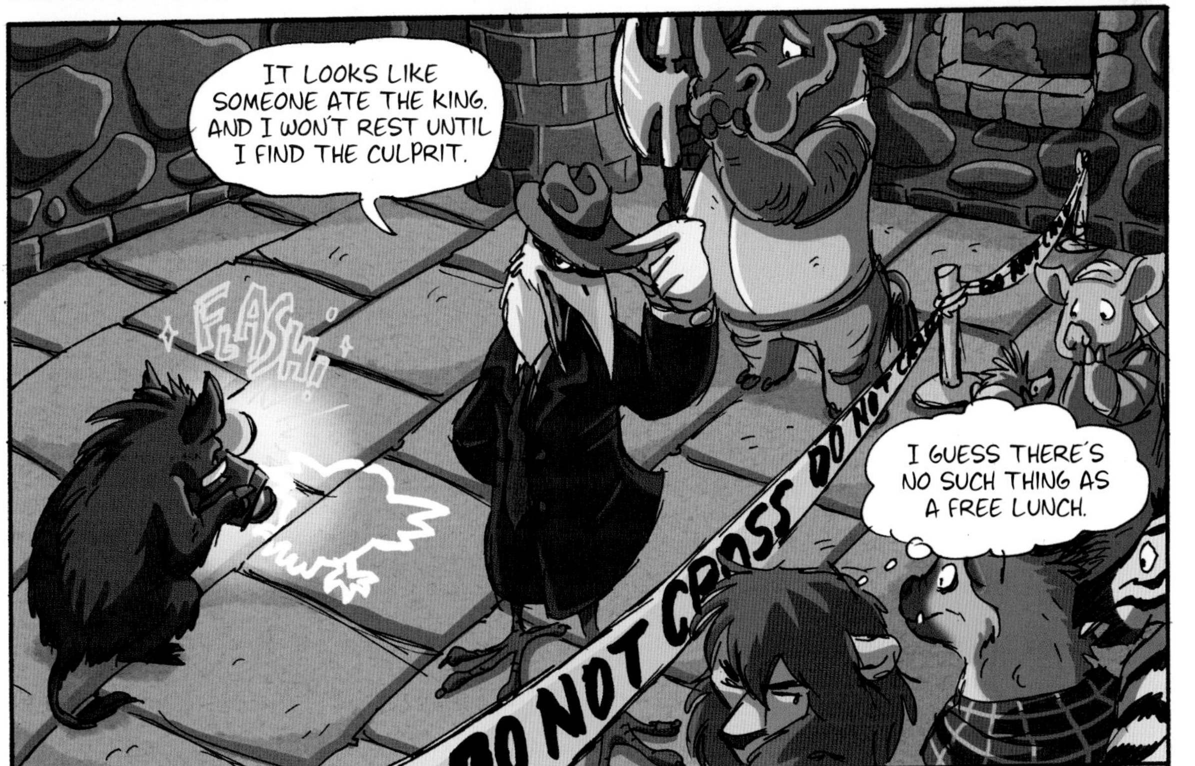
IT LOOKS LIKE SOMEONE ATE THE KING. AND I WON'T REST UNTIL I FIND THE CULPRIT.
FLASH!
I GUESS THERE'S NO SUCH THING AS A FREE LUNCH.
DO NOT CROSS

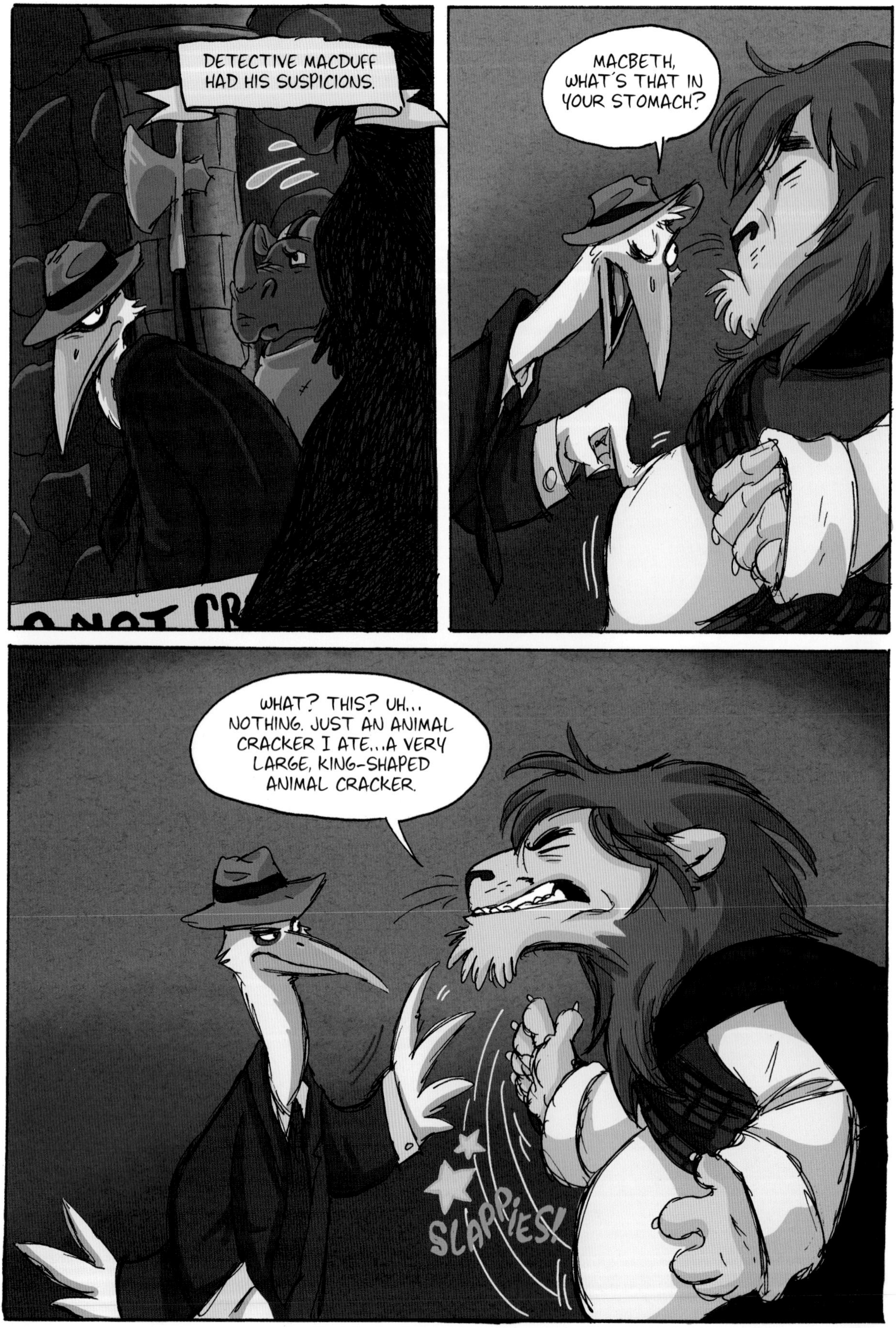
DETECTIVE MACDUFF HAD HIS SUSPICIONS.
MACBETH, WHAT'S THAT IN YOUR STOMACH?
WHAT? THIS? UH... NOTHING. JUST AN ANIMAL CRACKER I ATE...A VERY LARGE, KING-SHAPED ANIMAL CRACKER.
SLAPPIES!

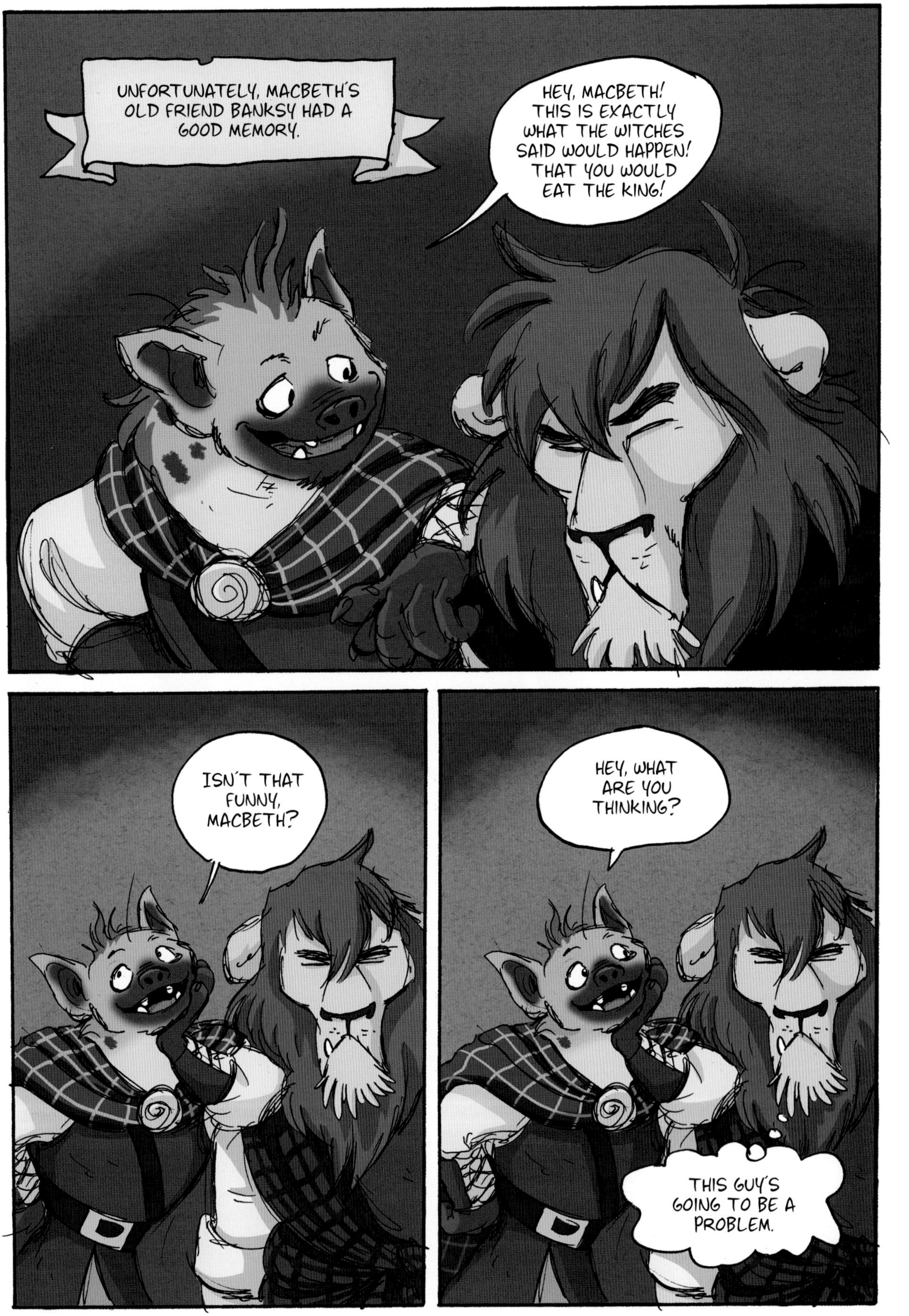
UNFORTUNATELY, MACBETH'S OLD FRIEND BANKSY HAD A GOOD MEMORY.
HEY, MACBETH! THIS IS EXACTLY WHAT THE WITCHES SAID WOULD HAPPEN! THAT YOU WOULD EAT THE KING!
ISN'T THAT FUNNY, MACBETH?
HEY, WHAT ARE YOU THINKING?
THIS GUY'S GOING TO BE A PROBLEM.

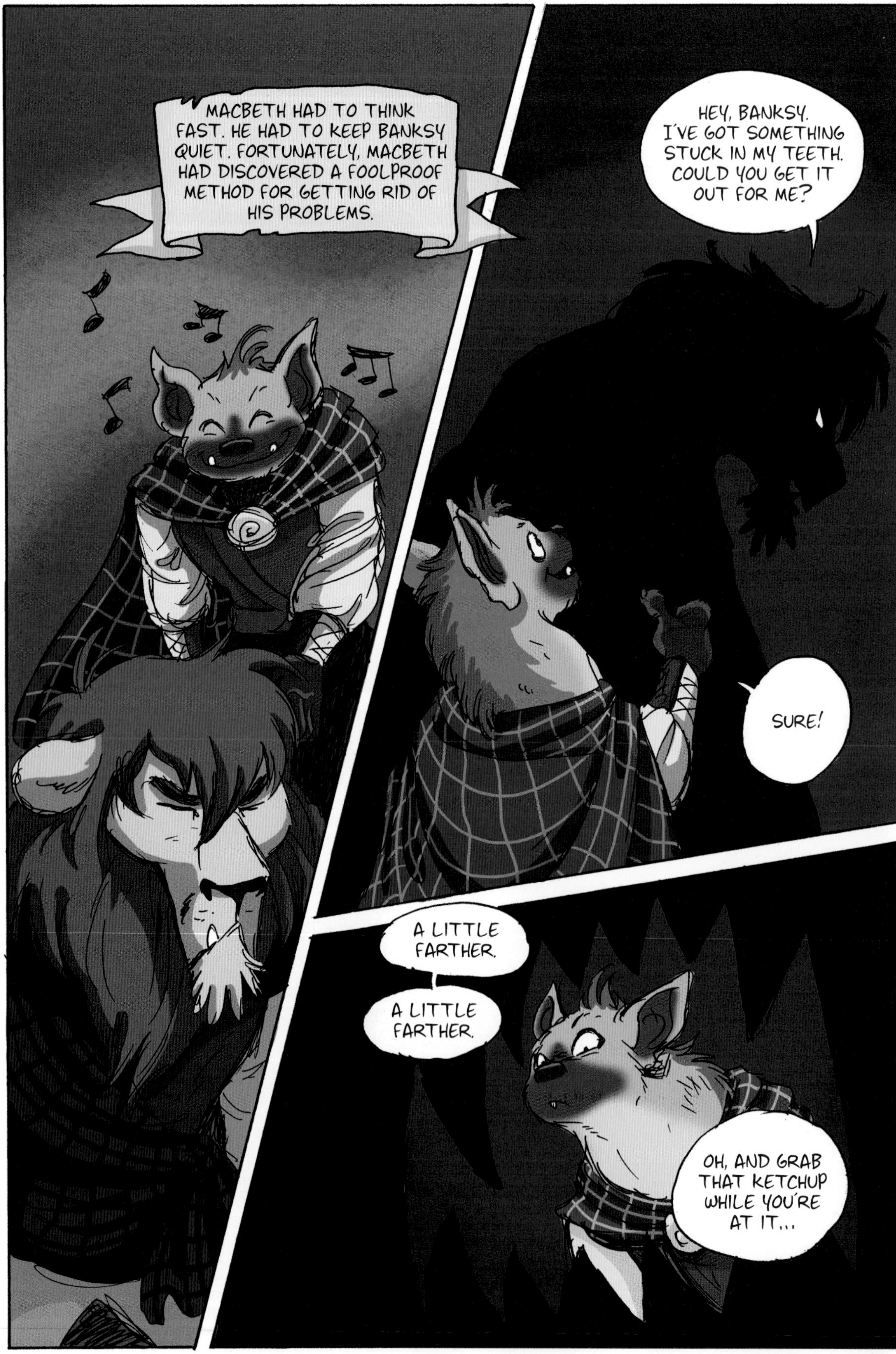
MACBETH HAD TO THINK FAST. HE HAD TO KEEP BANKSY QUIET. FORTUNATELY, MACBETH HAD DISCOVERED A FOOLPROOF METHOD FOR GETTING RID OF HIS PROBLEMS.
HEY, BANKSY. I'VE GOT SOMETHING STUCK IN MY TEETH. COULD YOU GET IT OUT FOR ME?
SURE!
A LITTLE FARTHER.
A LITTLE FARTHER.
OH, AND GRAB THAT KETCHUP WHILE YOU'RE AT IT...

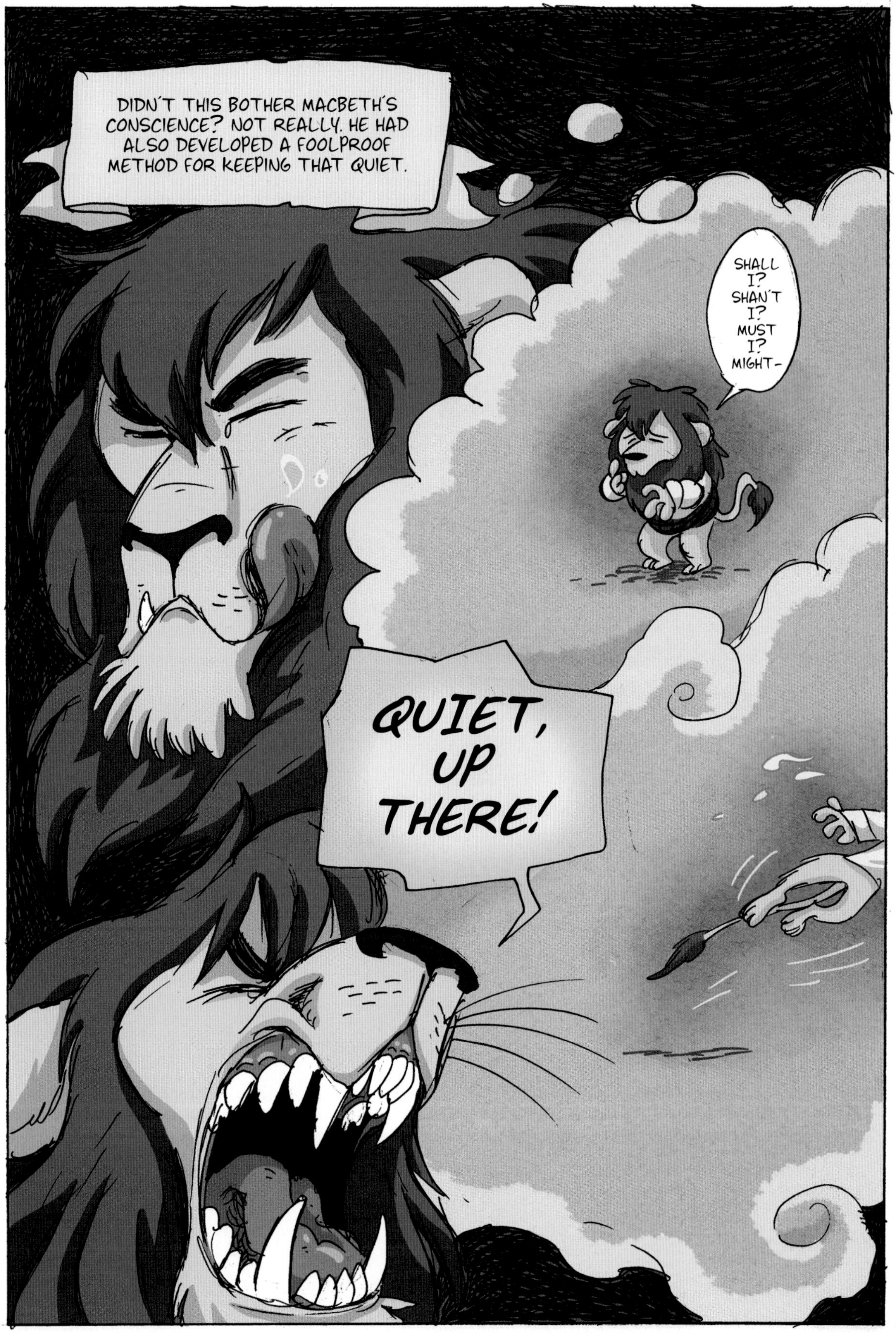
DIDN'T THIS BOTHER MACBETH'S CONSCIENCE? NOT REALLY. HE HAD ALSO DEVELOPED A FOOLPROOF METHOD FOR KEEPING THAT QUIET.
SHALL I? SHAN'T I? MUST I? MIGHT-
QUIET, UP THERE!

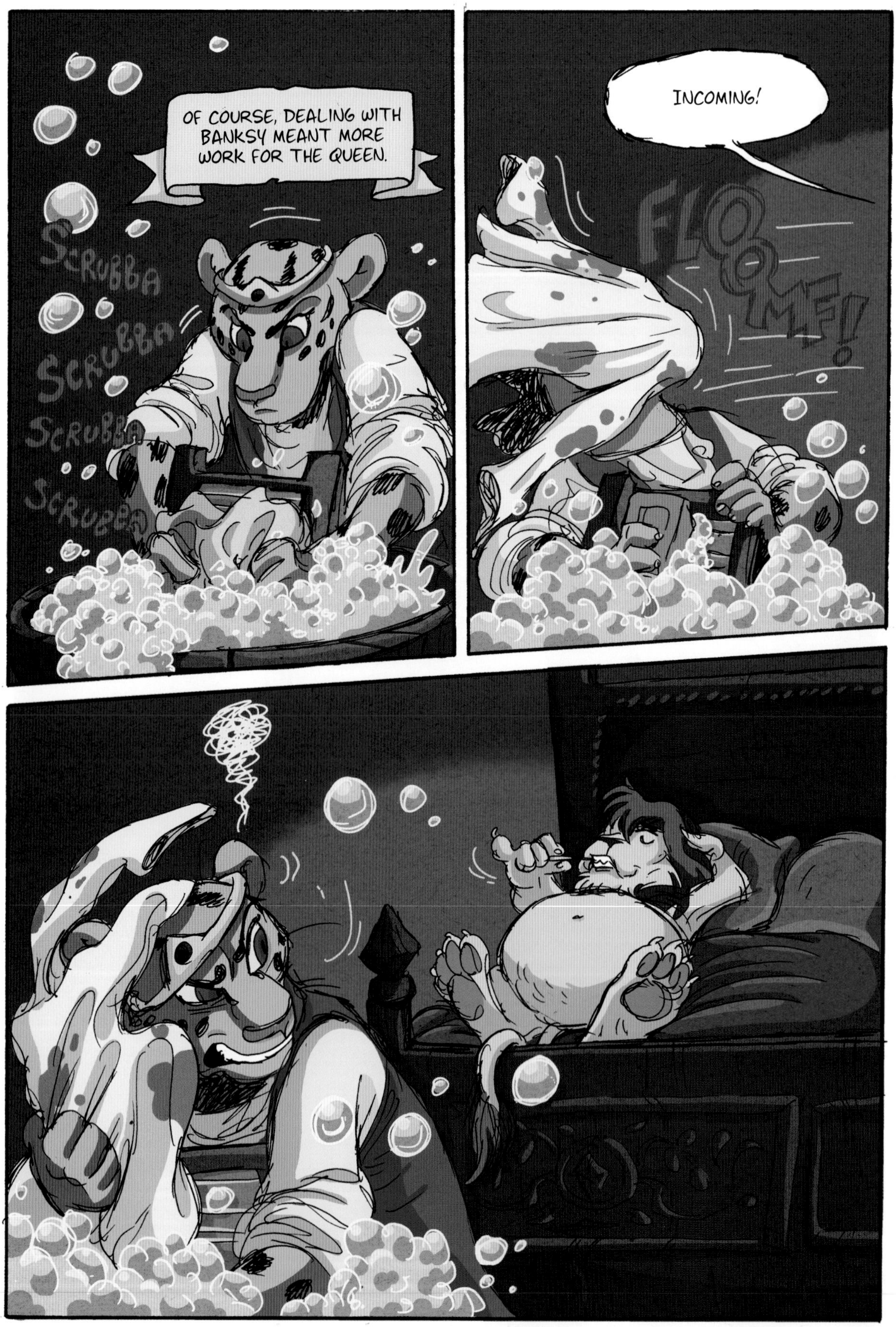
OF COURSE, DEALING WITH BANKSY MEANT MORE WORK FOR THE QUEEN.
SCRUBBA SCRUBBA SCRUBBA SCRUBBA SCRUBBA
INCOMING!
FLOOMF!

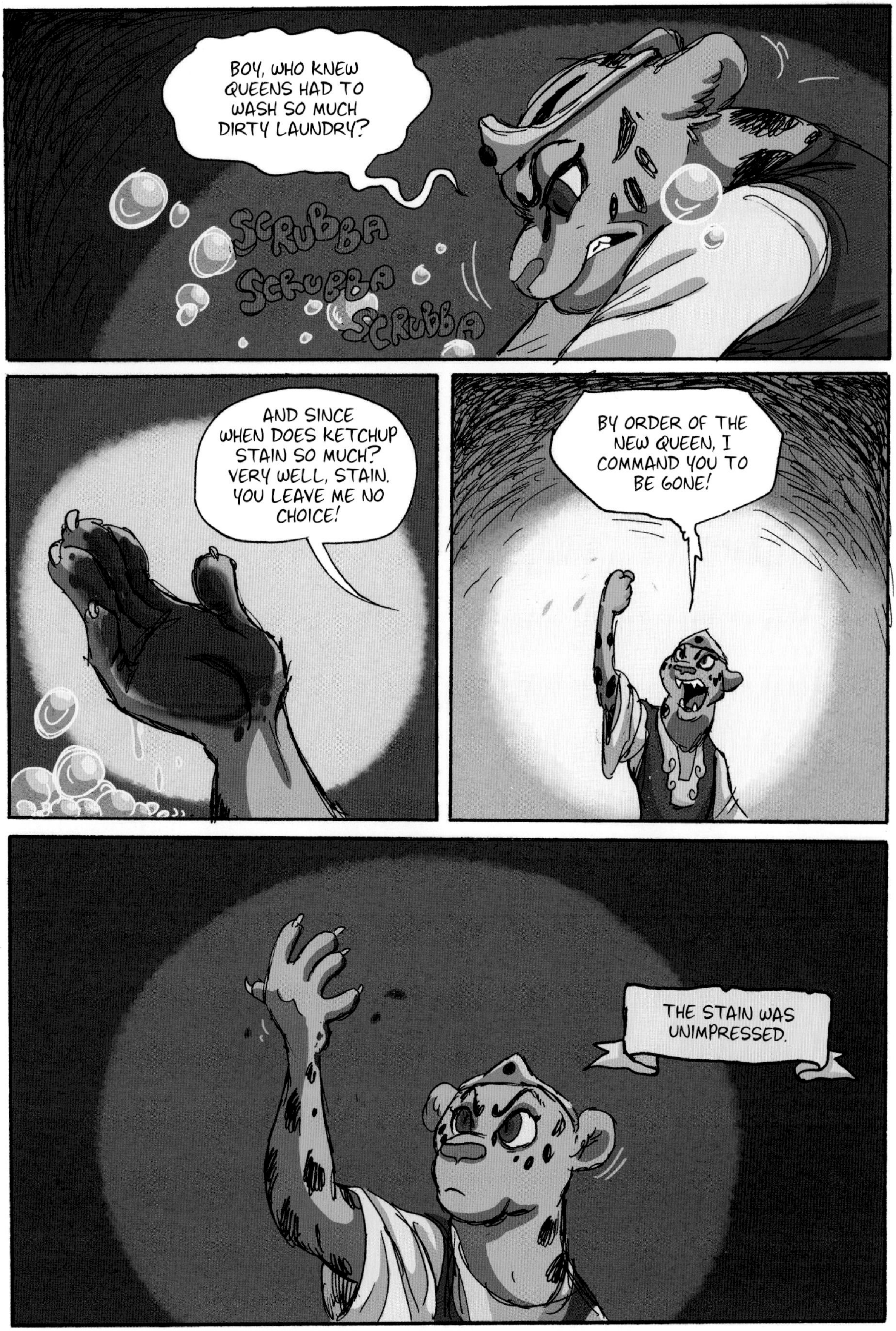
BOY, WHO KNEW QUEENS HAD TO WASH SO MUCH DIRTY LAUNDRY?
SCRUBBA SCRUBBA SCRUBBA
AND SINCE WHEN DOES KETCHUP STAIN SO MUCH? VERY WELL, STAIN. YOU LEAVE ME NO CHOICE!
BY ORDER OF THE NEW QUEEN, I COMMAND YOU TO BE GONE!
THE STAIN WAS UNIMPRESSED.

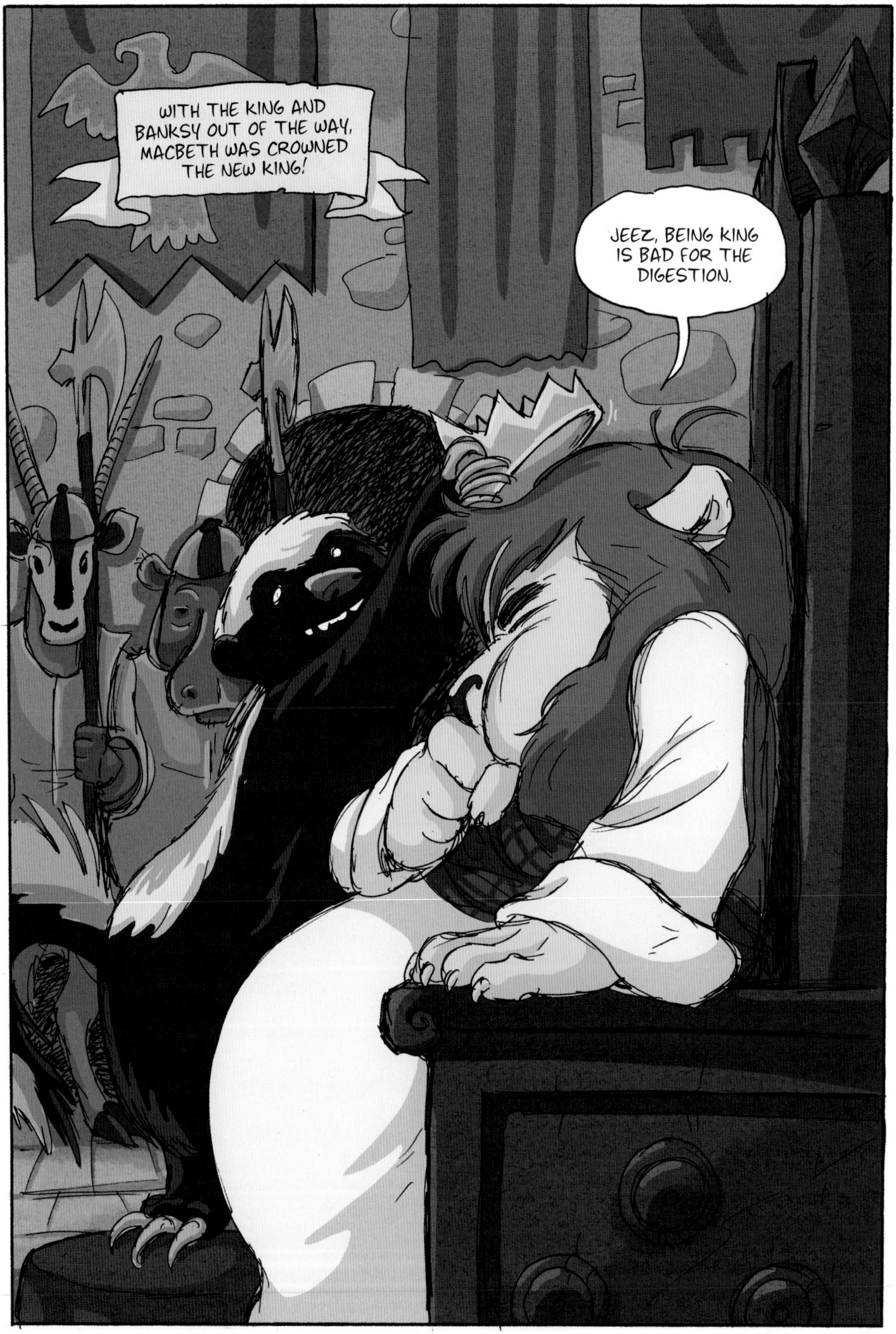
WITH THE KING AND BANKSY OUT OF THE WAY, MACBETH WAS CROWNED THE NEW KING!
JEEZ, BEING KING IS BAD FOR THE DIGESTION.

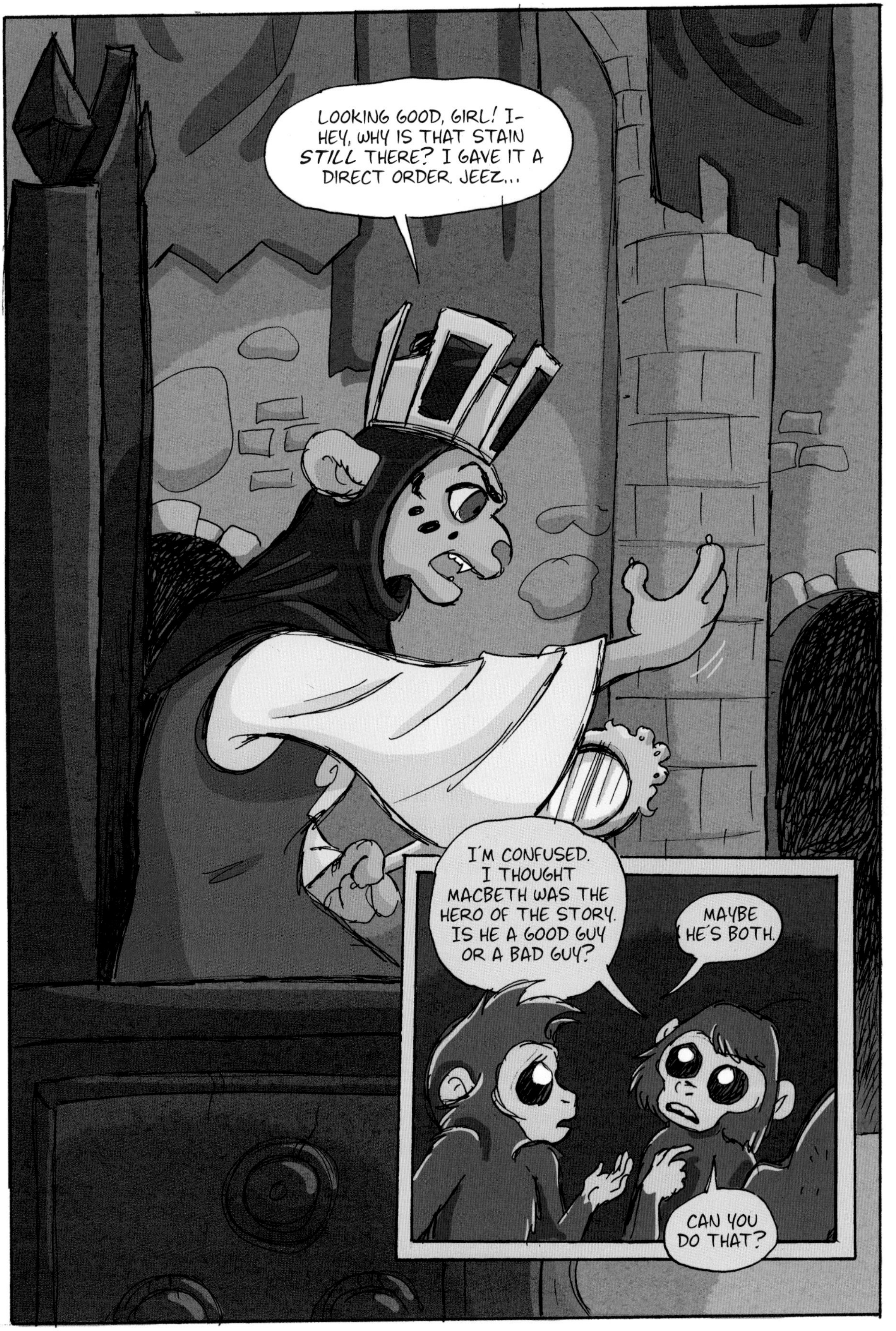
LOOKING GOOD, GIRL! I- HEY, WHY IS THAT STAIN STILL THERE? I GAVE IT A DIRECT ORDER. JEEZ...
I'M CONFUSED. I THOUGHT MACBETH WAS THE HERO OF THE STORY. IS HE A GOOD GUY OR A BAD GUY?
MAYBE HE'S BOTH.
CAN YOU DO THAT?

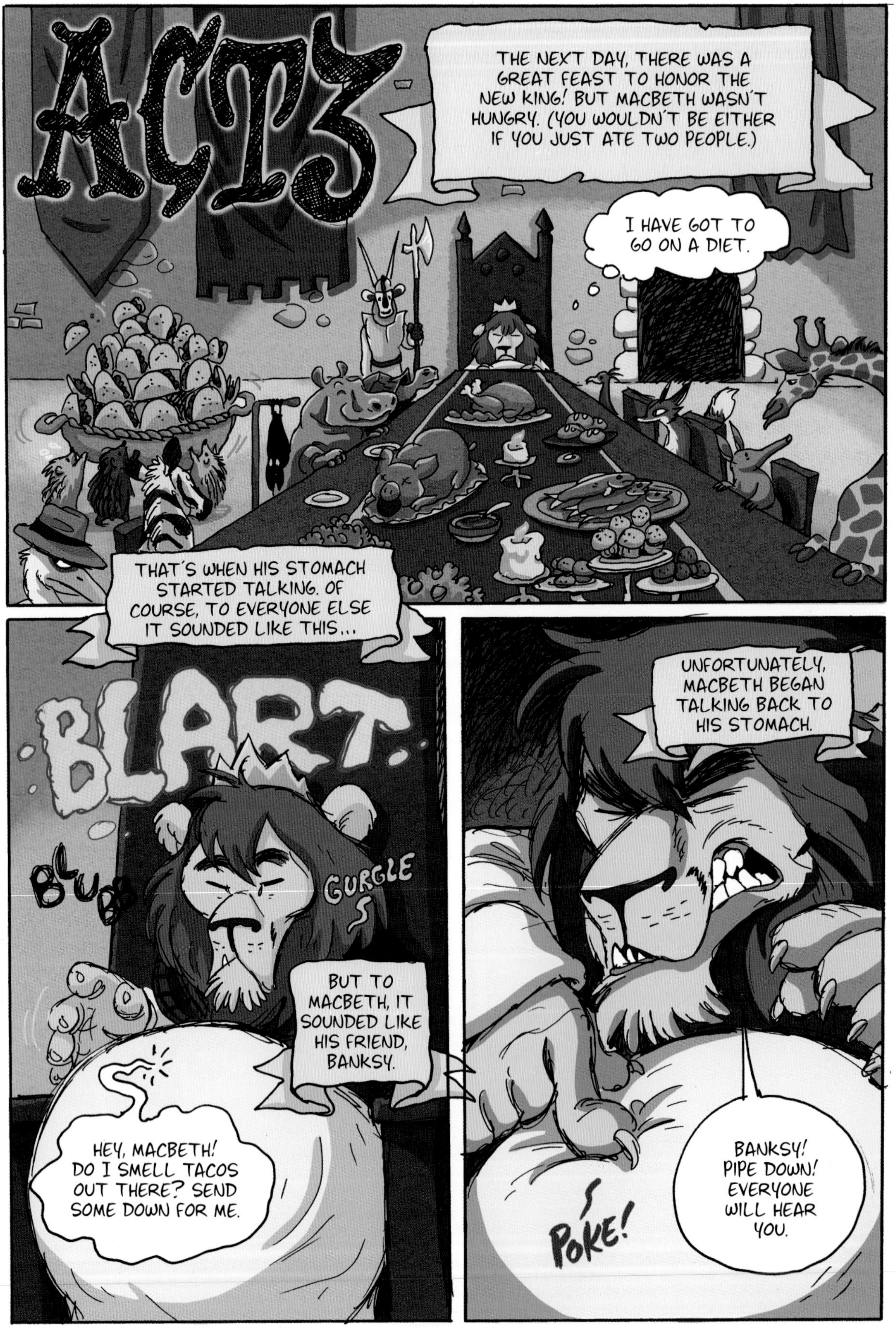
ACT 3
THE NEXT DAY, THERE WAS A GREAT FEAST TO HONOR THE NEW KING! BUT MACBETH WASN'T HUNGRY. (YOU WOULDN'T BE EITHER IF YOU JUST ATE TWO PEOPLE.)
I HAVE GOT TO GO ON A DIET.
THAT'S WHEN HIS STOMACH STARTED TALKING. OF COURSE, TO EVERYONE ELSE IT SOUNDED LIKE THIS...
BLART.
BLUBB
GURGLE
BUT TO MACBETH, IT SOUNDED LIKE HIS FRIEND, BANKSY.
HEY, MACBETH! DO I SMELL TACOS OUT THERE? SEND SOME DOWN FOR ME.
UNFORTUNATELY, MACBETH BEGAN TALKING BACK TO HIS STOMACH.
POKE!
BANKSY! PIPE DOWN! EVERYONE WILL HEAR YOU.

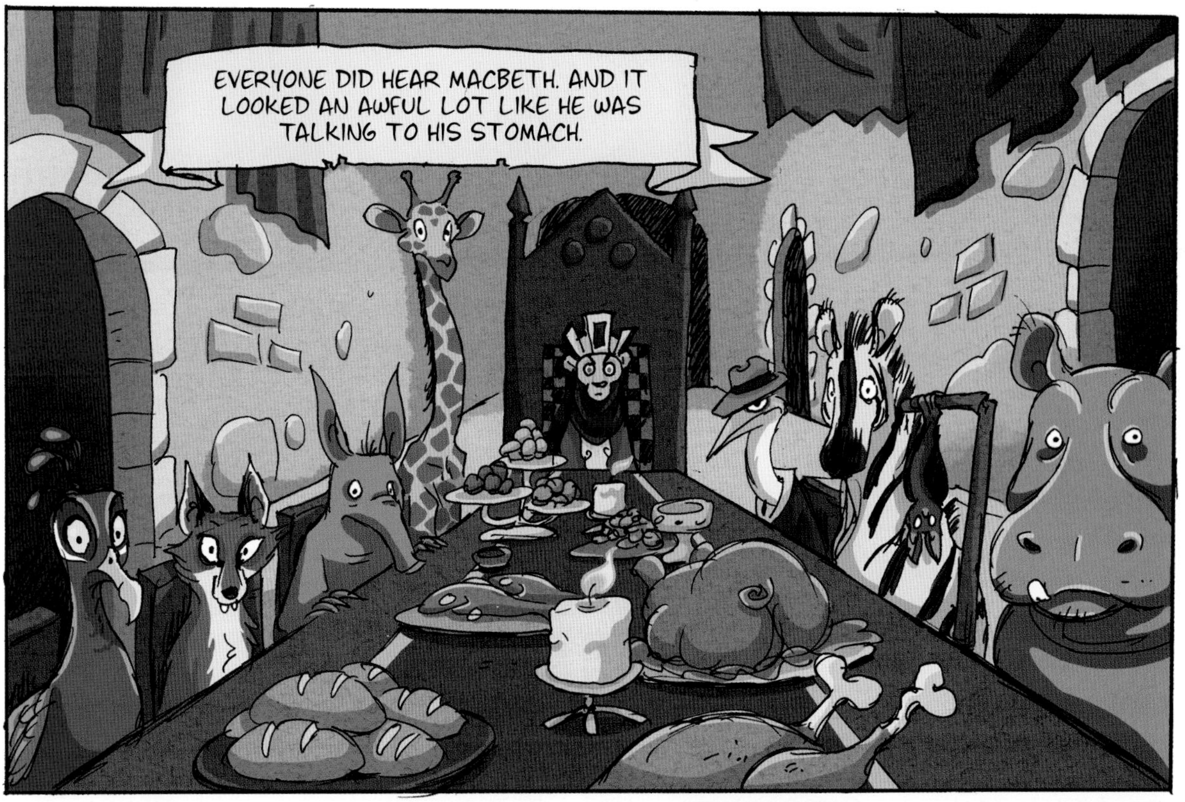
EVERYONE DID HEAR MACBETH. AND IT LOOKED AN AWFUL LOT LIKE HE WAS TALKING TO HIS STOMACH.

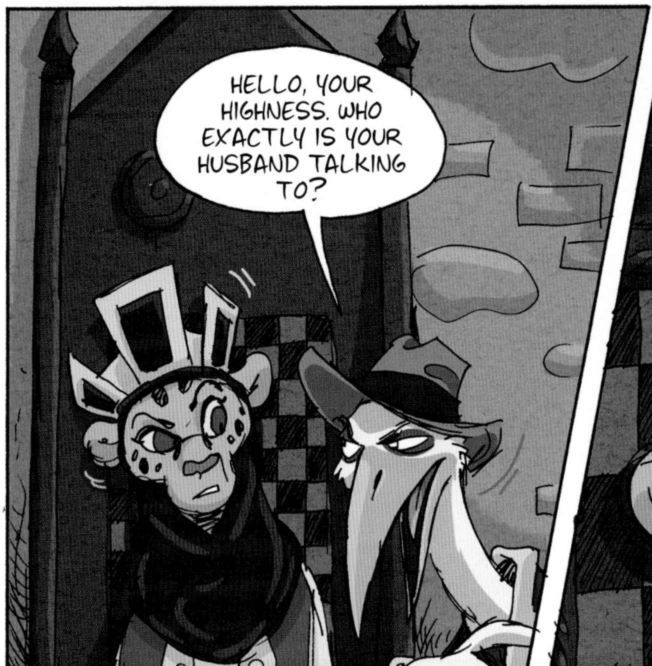
HELLO, YOUR HIGHNESS. WHO EXACTLY IS YOUR HUSBAND TALKING TO?

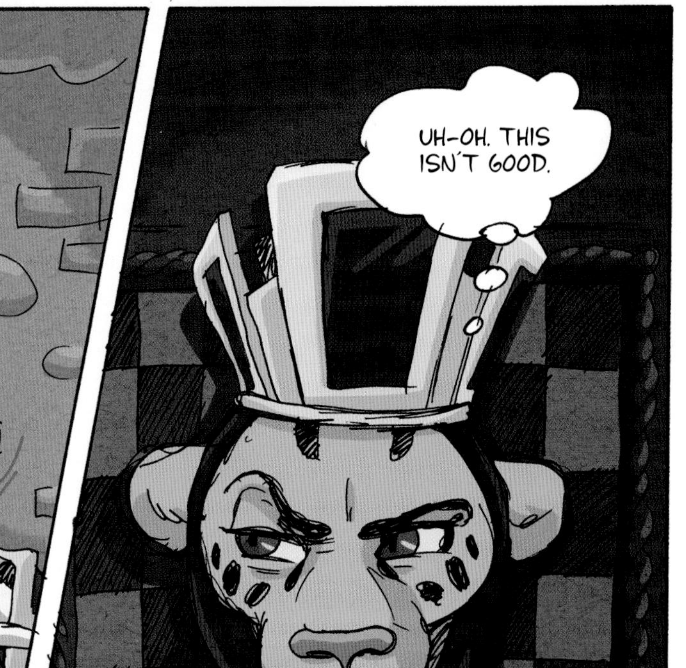
UH-OH. THIS ISN'T GOOD.

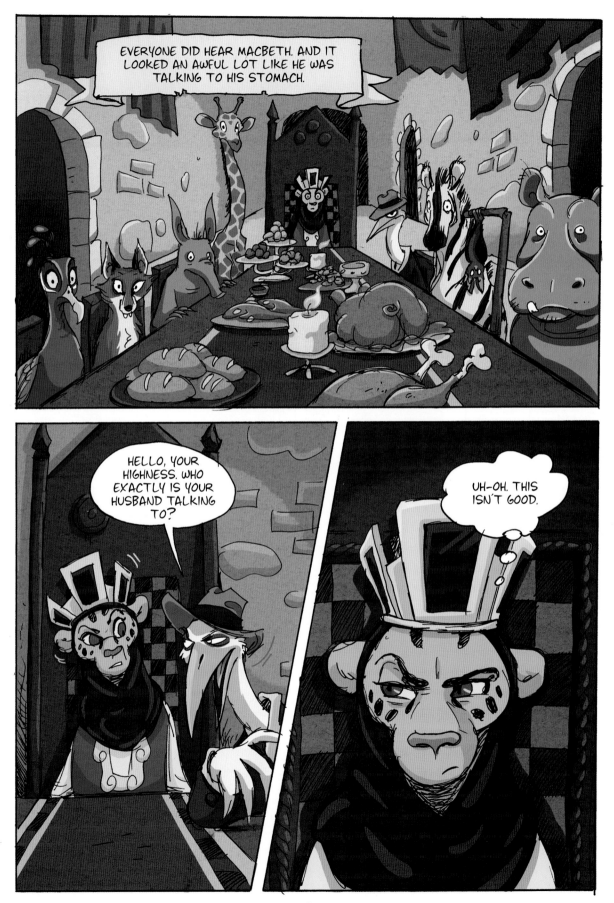

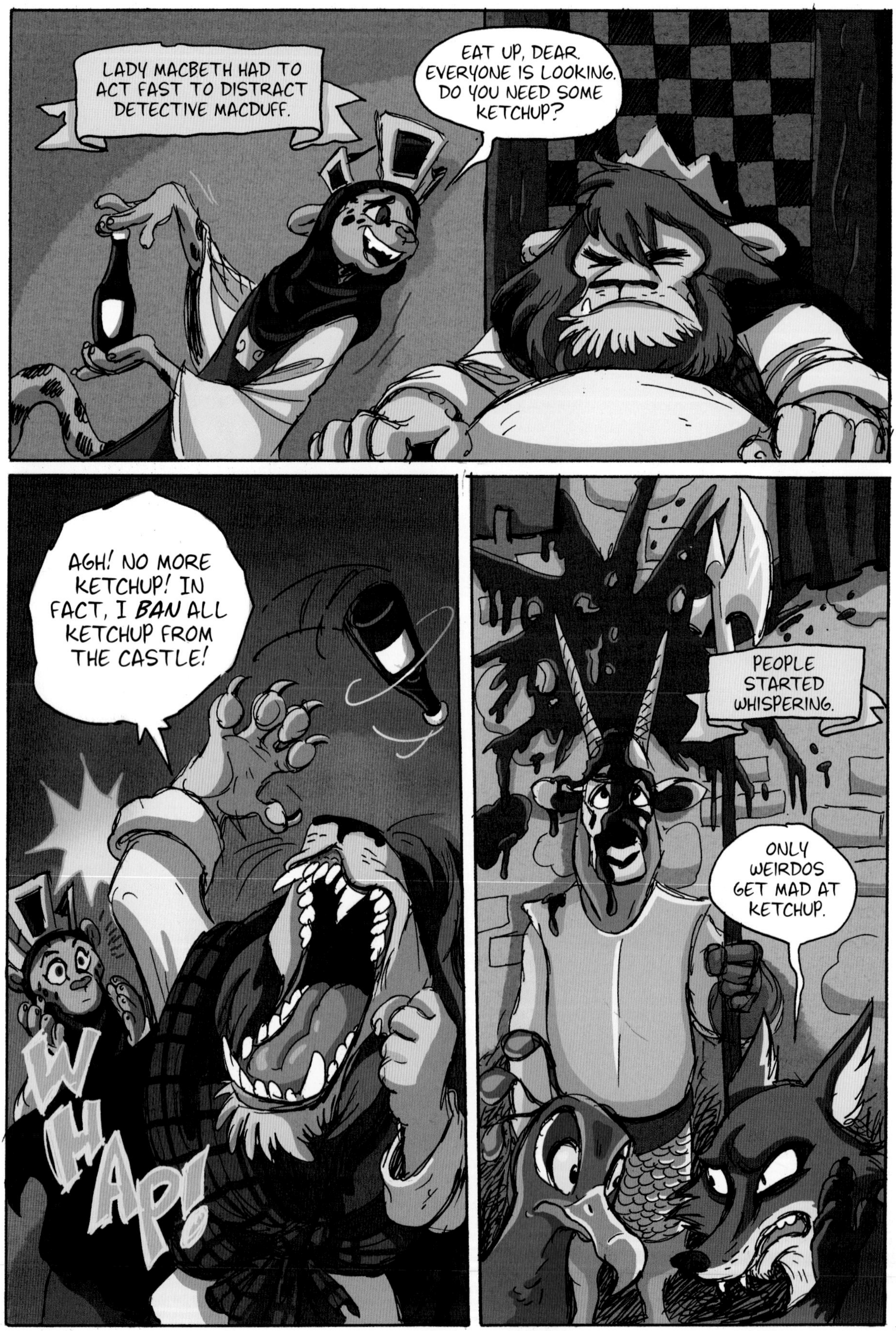
LADY MACBETH HAD TO ACT FAST TO DISTRACT DETECTIVE MACDUFF.
EAT UP, DEAR. EVERYONE IS LOOKING. DO YOU NEED SOME KETCHUP?
AGH! NO MORE KETCHUP! IN FACT, I *BAN* ALL KETCHUP FROM THE CASTLE!
WHAP!
PEOPLE STARTED WHISPERING.
ONLY WEIRDOS GET MAD AT KETCHUP.

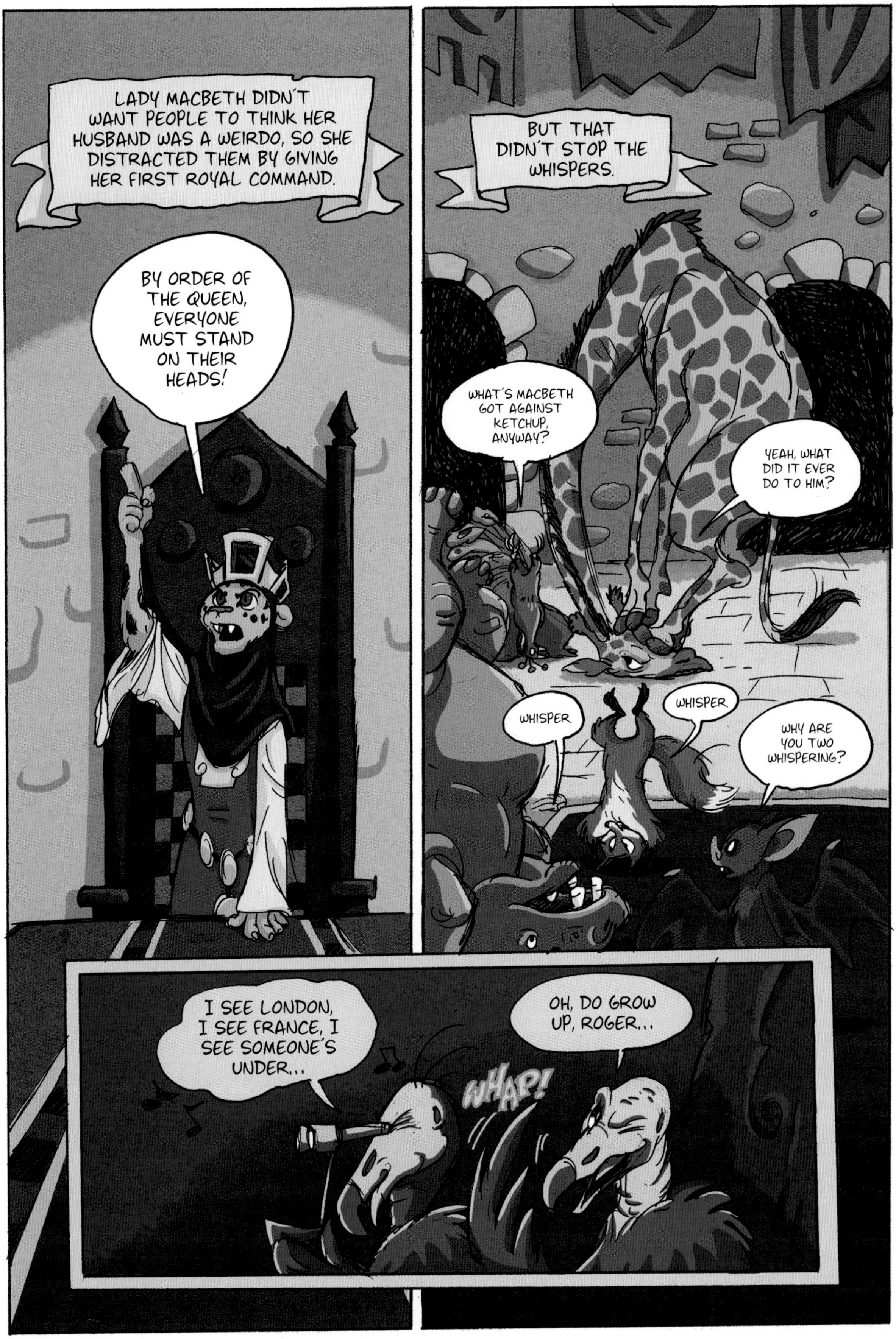
LADY MACBETH DIDN´T WANT PEOPLE TO THINK HER HUSBAND WAS A WEIRDO, SO SHE DISTRACTED THEM BY GIVING HER FIRST ROYAL COMMAND.
BY ORDER OF THE QUEEN, EVERYONE MUST STAND ON THEIR HEADS!
BUT THAT DIDN´T STOP THE WHISPERS.
WHAT´S MACBETH GOT AGAINST KETCHUP, ANYWAY?
YEAH, WHAT DID IT EVER DO TO HIM?
WHISPER.
WHISPER.
WHY ARE YOU TWO WHISPERING?
I SEE LONDON, I SEE FRANCE, I SEE SOMEONE´S UNDER...
OH, DO GROW UP, ROGER...
WHAP!

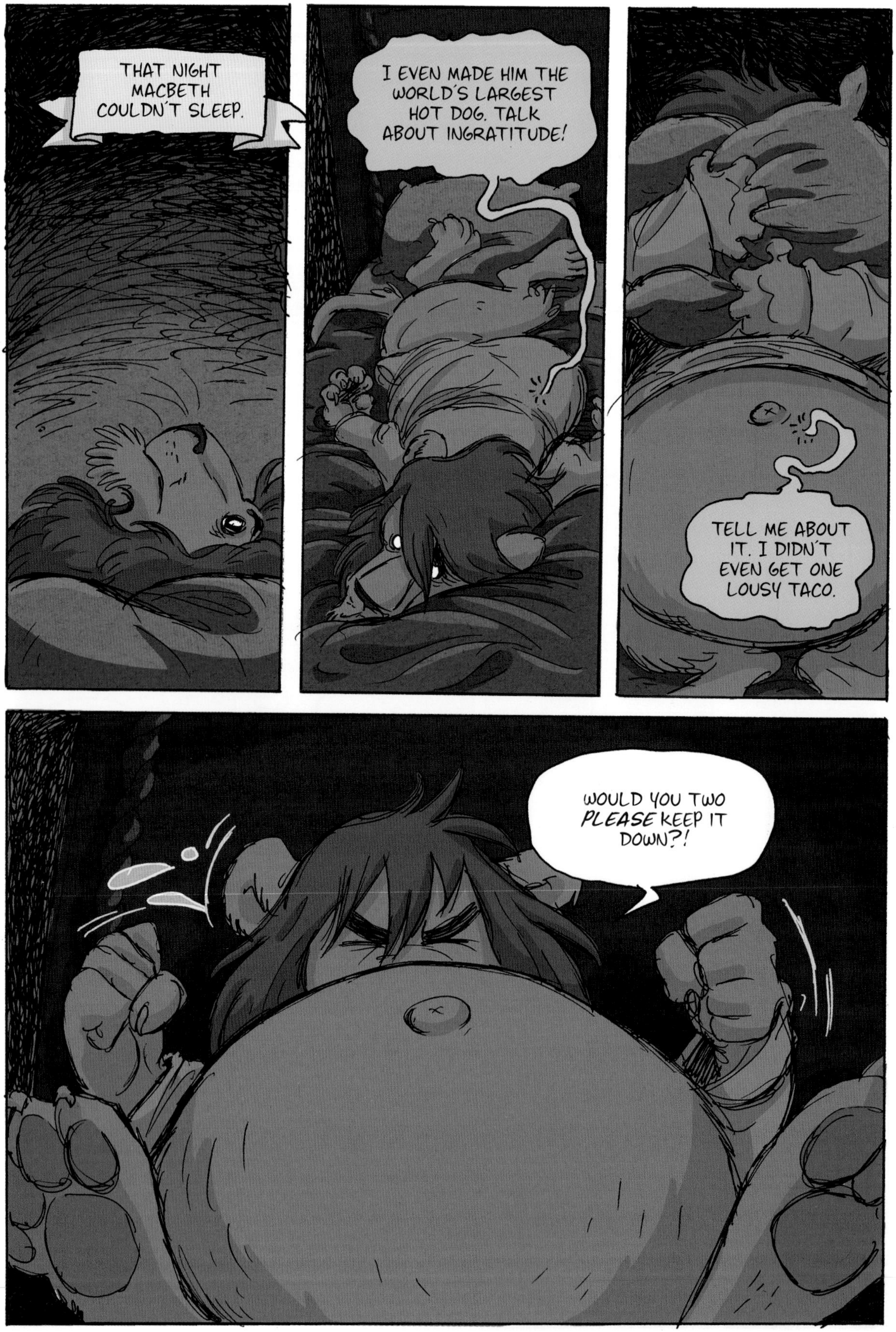
THAT NIGHT MACBETH COULDN'T SLEEP.
I EVEN MADE HIM THE WORLD'S LARGEST HOT DOG. TALK ABOUT INGRATITUDE!
TELL ME ABOUT IT. I DIDN'T EVEN GET ONE LOUSY TACO.
WOULD YOU TWO *PLEASE* KEEP IT DOWN?!

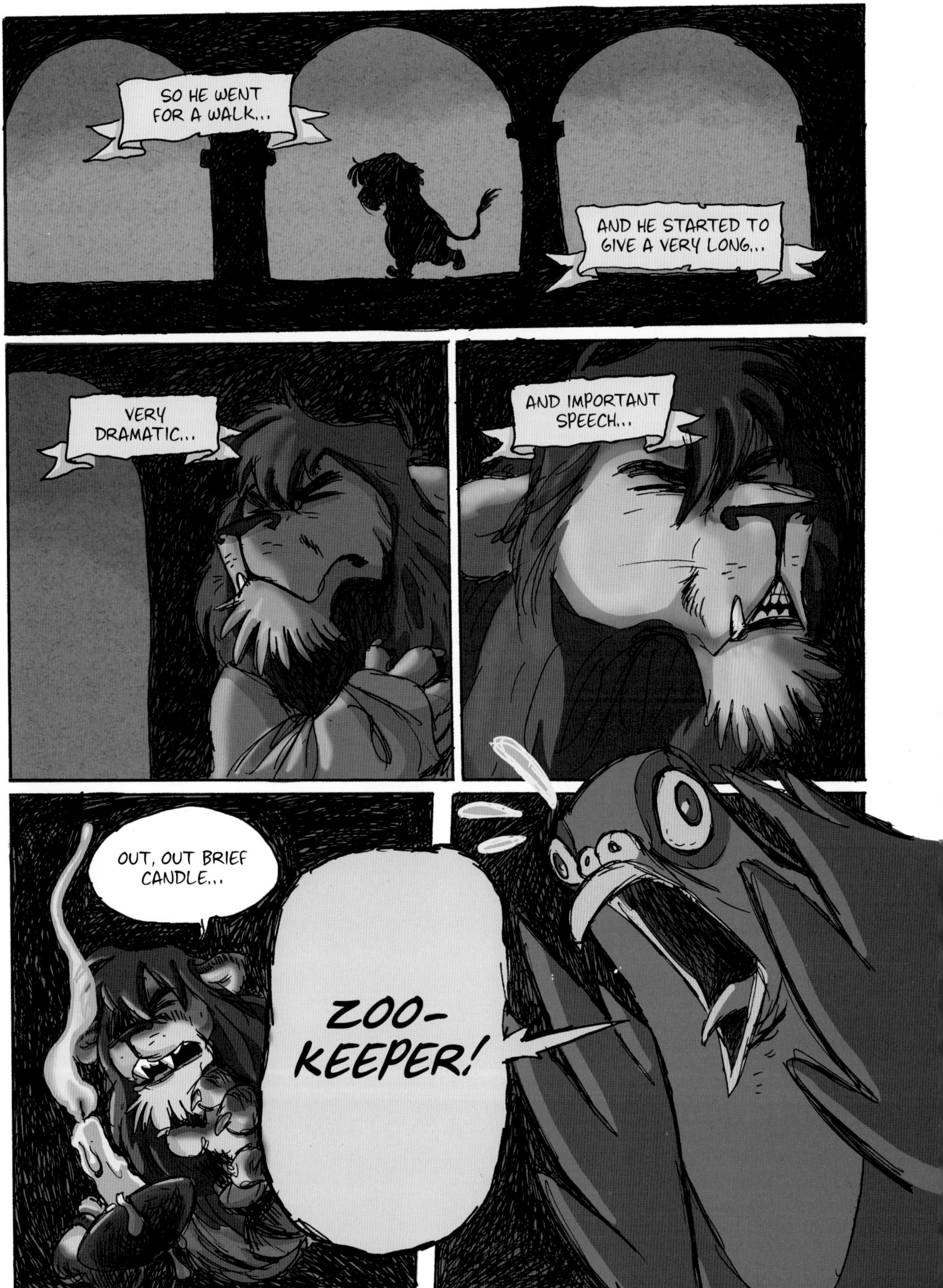
SO HE WENT FOR A WALK...
AND HE STARTED TO GIVE A VERY LONG...
VERY DRAMATIC...
AND IMPORTANT SPEECH...
OUT, OUT BRIEF CANDLE...
ZOO-KEEPER!

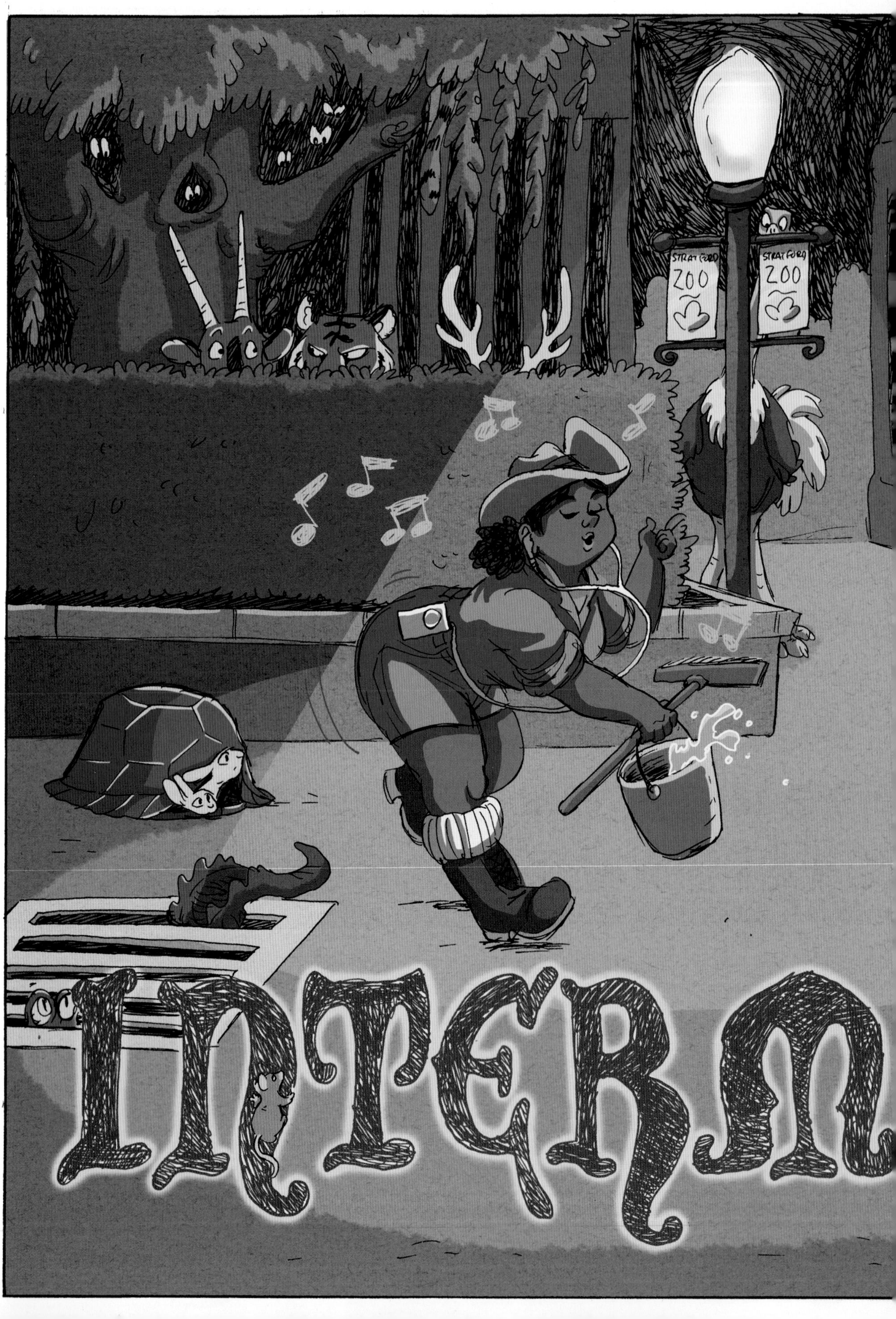
STRATFORD ZOO
STRATFORD ZOO
INTERM

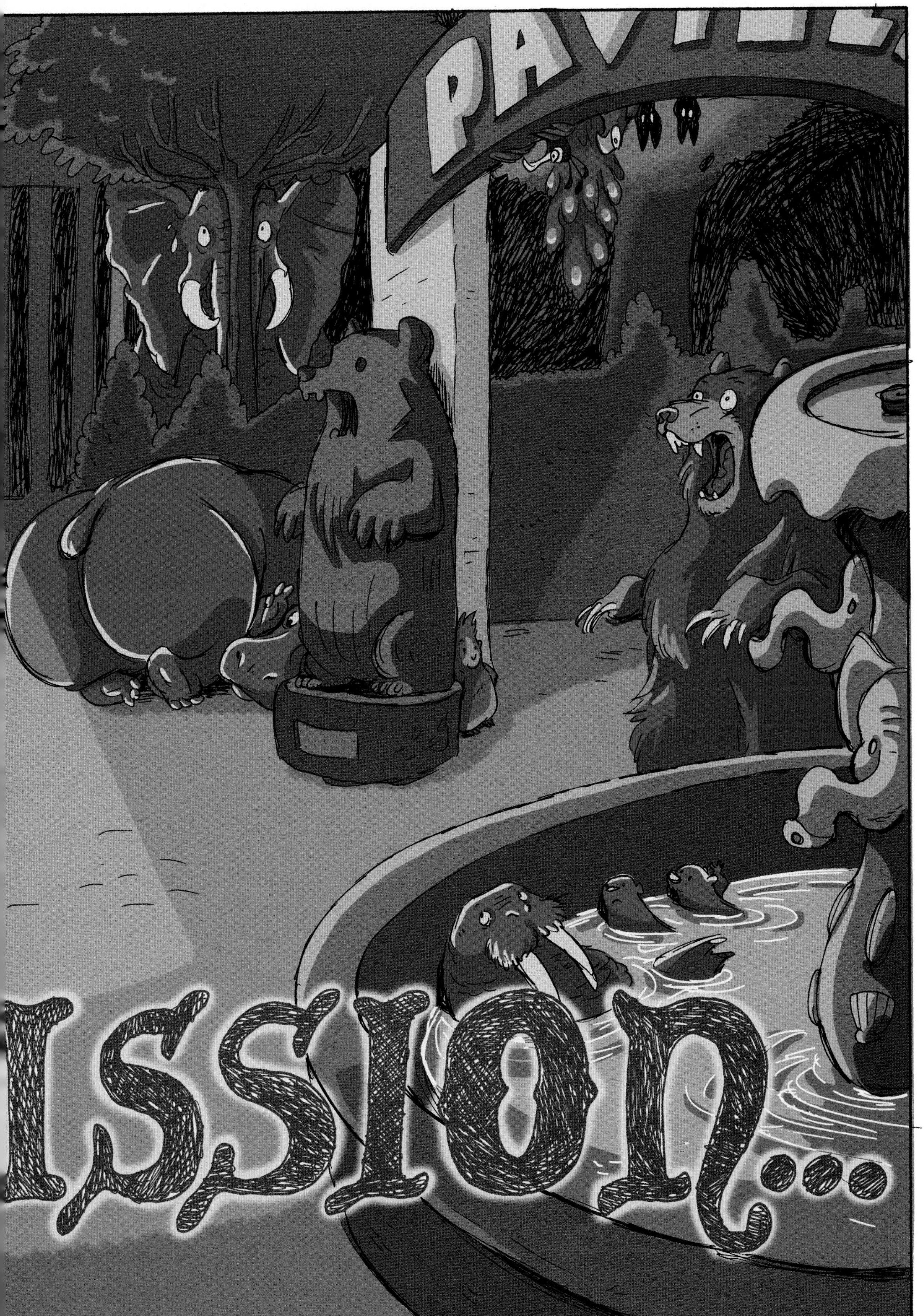
PAV
ission...

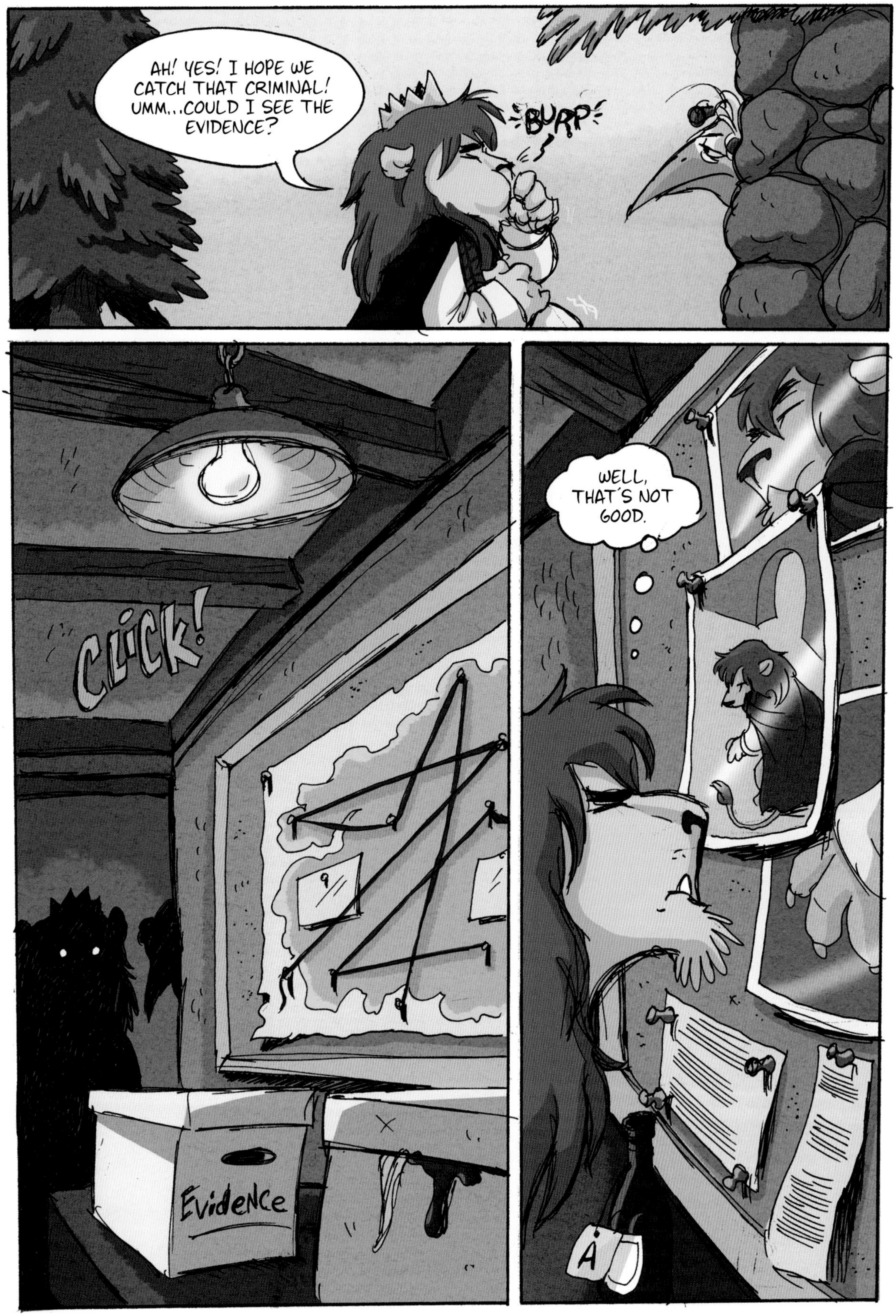
AH! YES! I HOPE WE CATCH THAT CRIMINAL! UMM...COULD I SEE THE EVIDENCE?
BURP
CLICK!
Evidence
WELL, THAT´S NOT GOOD.
A

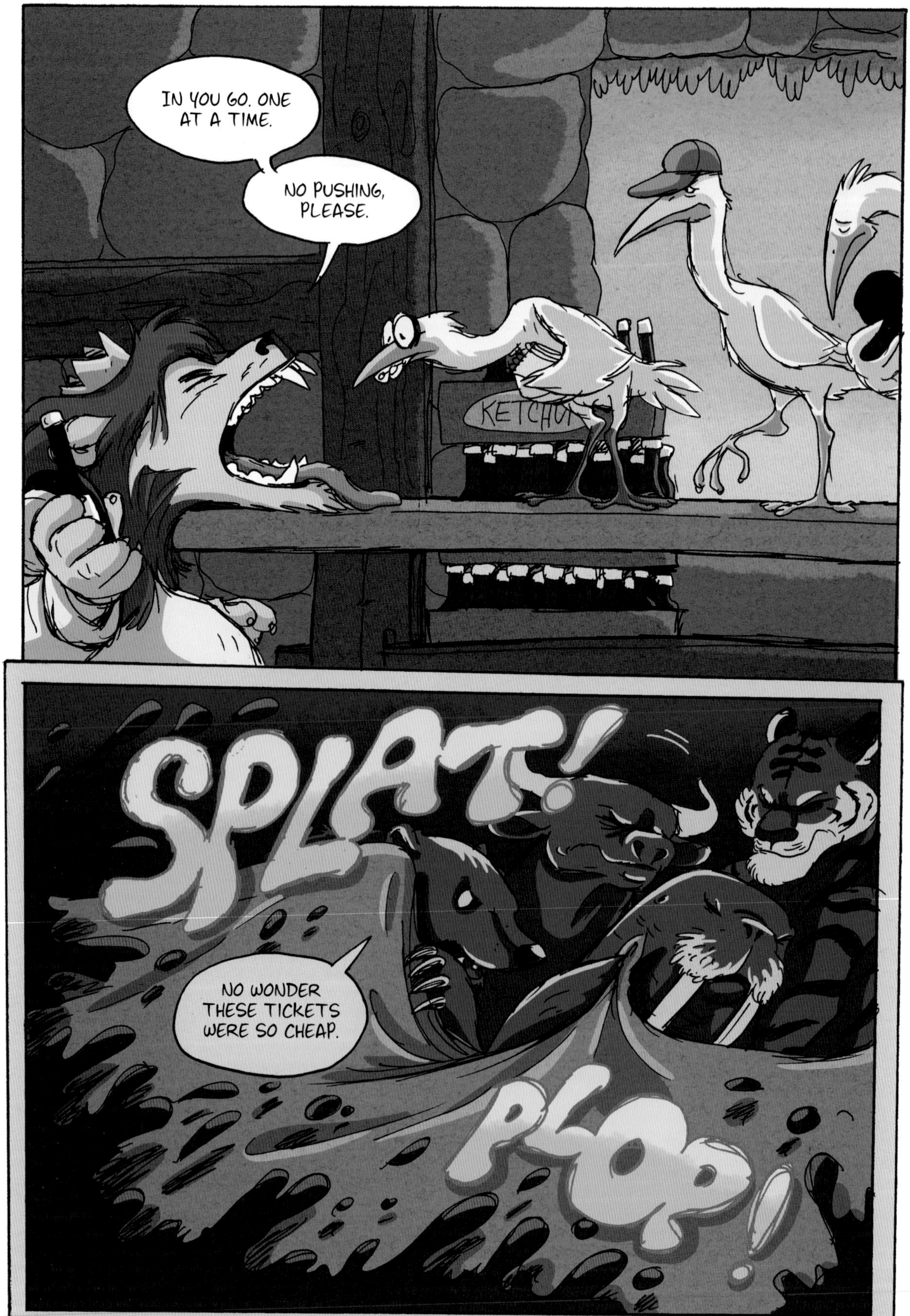
IN YOU GO. ONE AT A TIME.
NO PUSHING, PLEASE.
KETCHUP
SPLAT!
NO WONDER THESE TICKETS WERE SO CHEAP.
PLOP!

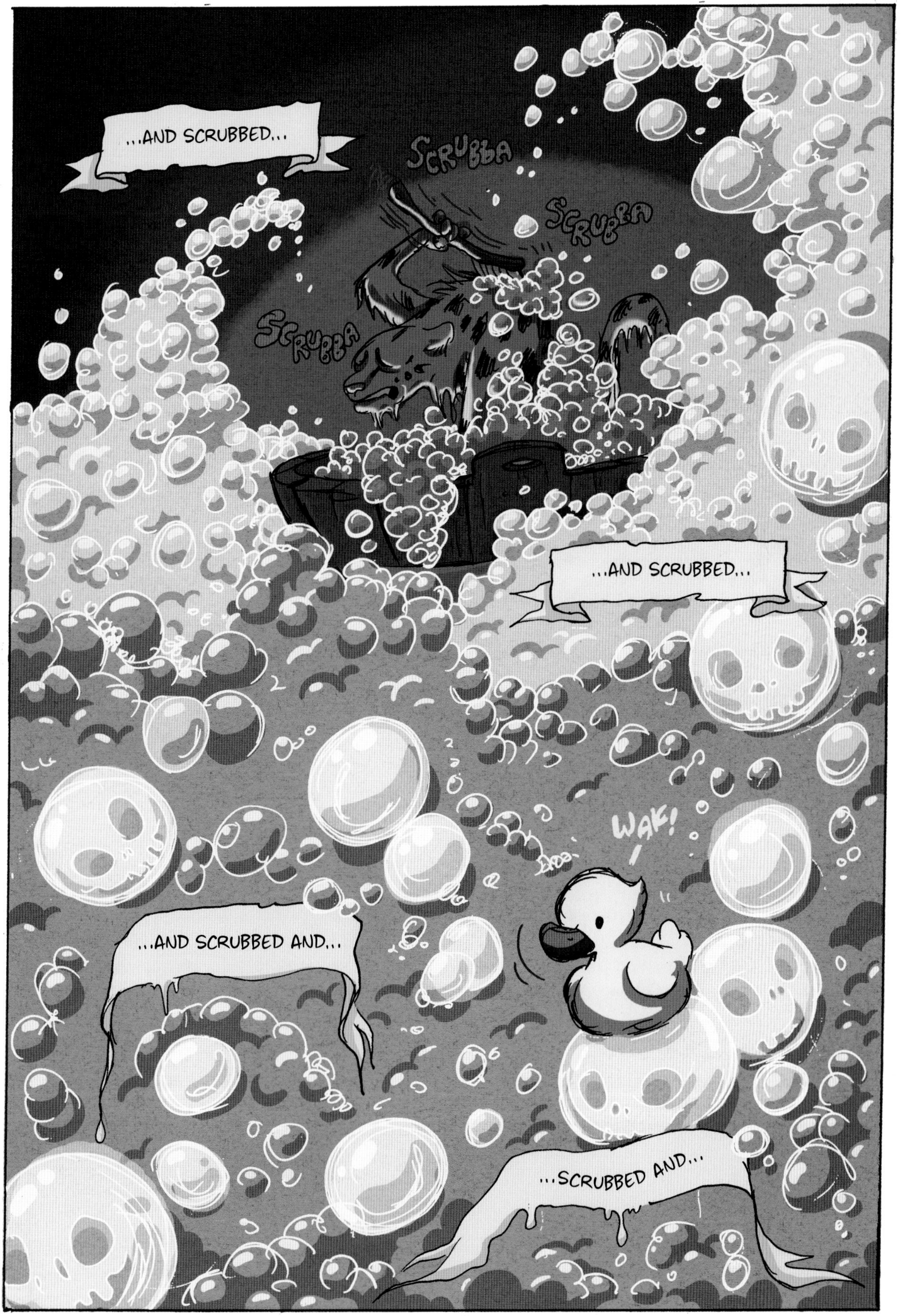
...AND SCRUBBED...
SCRUBBA
SCRUBBA
SCRUBBA
...AND SCRUBBED...
WAK!
...AND SCRUBBED AND...
...SCRUBBED AND...

64

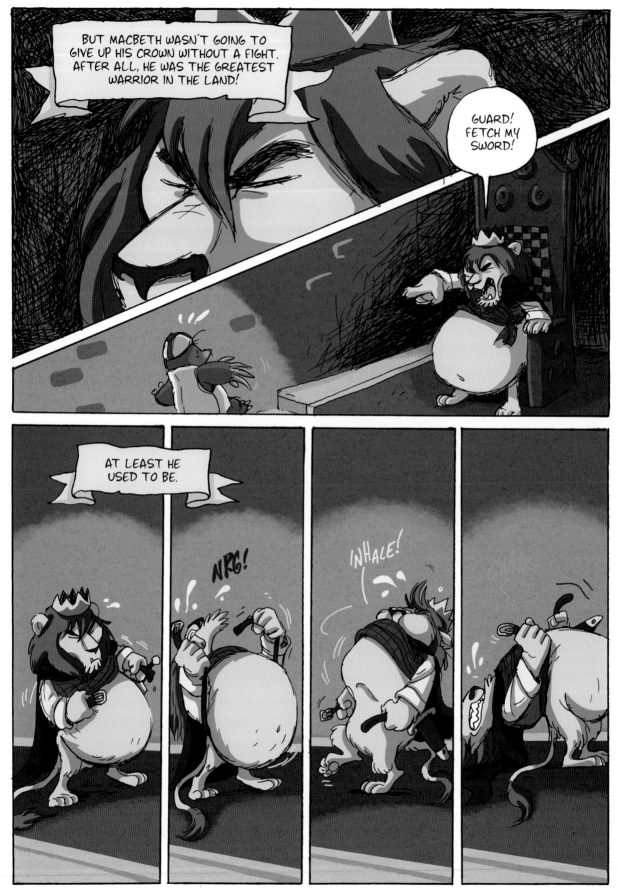

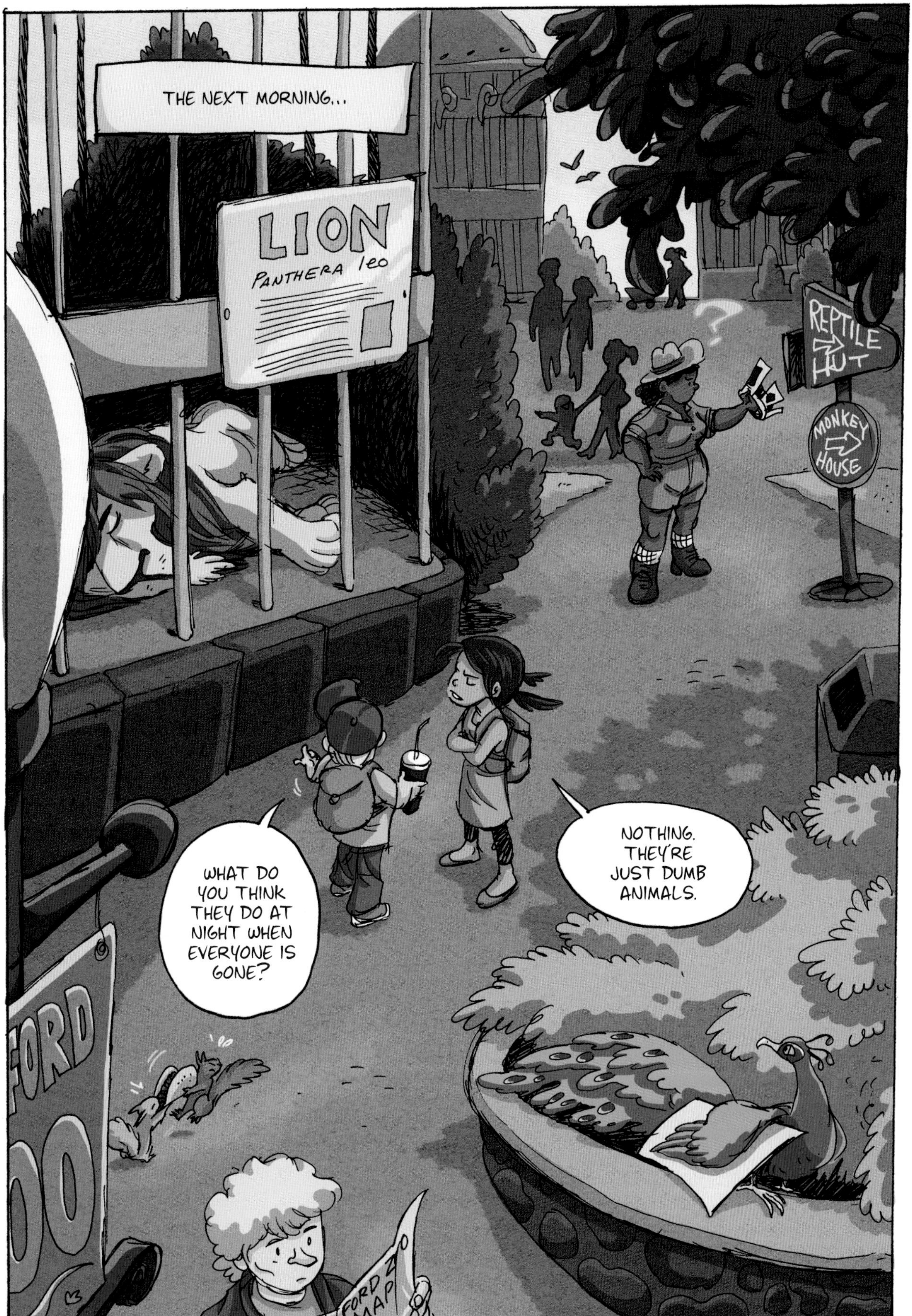
THE NEXT MORNING...
LION
PANTHERA leo
REPTILE HUT
MONKEY HOUSE
WHAT DO YOU THINK THEY DO AT NIGHT WHEN EVERYONE IS GONE?
NOTHING. THEY'RE JUST DUMB ANIMALS.
FORD
FORD ZO MAP

First Second

Published by First Second
First Second is an imprint of Roaring Brook Press,
a division of Holtzbrinck Publishing Holdings Limited Partnership
175 Fifth Avenue, New York, New York 10010

Cataloging-in-Publication Data is on file at the Library of Congress.

Hardcover ISBN 978-1-62672-101-2
Paperback ISBN 978-1-59643-915-3

FIRST
EDITION

First edition 2014
Book design by Colleen AF Venable
Colors by Alisa Harris

Printed in China by Toppan Leefung Printing Ltd, Dongguan City, Guangdong Province

Hardcover: 10 9 8 7 6 5 4 3 2 1
Paperback: 10 9 8 7 6 5 4 3 2 1